A BEAD IN THE HAND

A Glass Bead Mystery

JANICE PEACOCK

Vetrai Press

Lafayette, California

2016

First published in 2015 by Booktrope: *A Bead in the Hand, A Glass Bead Mystery, Book 2*
Published in 2016 by Vetrai Press: *A Bead in the Hand, A Glass Bead Mystery, Book 2*

Cover Design by Greg Simanson
Edited by Ellen Margulies

This is a work of fiction. Names, characters, places, brands, media, and incidents are either the product of the author's imagination or are used fictitiously. Any resemblance to similarly named places or to persons living or deceased is unintentional.

Print ISBN 978-0-9905705-6-1

For Mom

BOOKS BY JANICE PEACOCK

High Strung, Glass Bead Mystery Series, Book One

A Bead in the Hand, Glass Bead Mystery Series, Book Two

Off the Beadin' Path, Glass Bead Mystery Series, Book Three

Be Still My Beading Heart, A Glass Bead Mini-Mystery

ONE

THE WEEKEND GOT OFF to a bad start when I stepped on Gumdrop. It went from bad to tragic when I held a woman in my arms and knew there was no way I could save her. She was already dead.

· · ·

I was standing on my tallest stool, reaching to grab the last tray of beads from the top shelf in the guest room closet.

"Almost...got...it," I said to my cat Gumdrop, who was watching me from the bed.

Finally, I hooked my fingernails on the edge of the tray and pulled it slowly off the shelf, careful not to spill the contents of the shallow box. In preparation for an upcoming sale, I had placed each bead into its own separate spot in the grid of compartments in the tray. I took a slow step down one of the rungs of the stool, then another. Relieved that I was almost down, I took my final step toward the floor and realized—too late—I'd stepped on Gumdrop. The ear-piercing screech of a pissed-off cat threw me off balance— that, of course, and the fact that I was not stepping on the floor, but instead on the body of a cat who was attempting to flee. I tried to regain my balance, but it was a lost cause. With one last futile leap, I tried to stick a perfect 10-point landing, gymnast-style, holding the tray above my head. I saw myself falling in slow motion, the tray of glass beads still in my hands, as I plunged to the floor. The beads left the tray and went flying through the air. It was bad enough that they were falling, and possibly breaking, but it was a real insult that they were pelting down on my head like hail.

"Dammit, Gummie, why are you always in the way?" I yelled at Gumdrop, who had run from the room as fast as his fat body could carry him. I'd find him later, likely jammed under a pillow on the sofa, to sleep off the scary experience.

"Ouch," I added to no one but myself, feeling for lumps on my head.

Searching the Oriental carpet in my office-cum-guestroom, I tried to find all of the beads that had been flung from the tray by my not-so-graceful fall. When I squeezed under the bed, a swirl of cat hair drifted past me. I made a mental note to run the vacuum cleaner under here the next time I tackled the housekeeping in my half of the duplex.

After examining each bead, I replaced it into its cubby in the tray. These were glass beads, ones I had made myself in a torch by melting different colors of glass together. Fortunately, all the beads seemed to have made it, having been cooled properly overnight after I'd completed each one. I'd found twenty-three of the beads, but there was one empty spot left in the tray. Where had that bead gone? Under the desk? No. Still in the closet? No. In the carpet's fringe? No.

The doorbell rang. Brushing Gumdrop's hair off my jeans, I trotted to the door. I needed to get out the duct tape and give myself a once-over to get rid of the fluff, but didn't bother. I didn't want Val to have to wait. A quick glimpse in the mirror confirmed that my mop of light brown hair was sticking out in every direction, as usual. Then I noticed something strange—a large blue bead, wedged tightly in my cleavage. The missing bead. What a relief to spare Val from seeing that. It spared me, too, from getting teased by her for weeks to follow.

I pulled open the front door.

"Eh uh en geh de doo ohen," my neighbor Val said, while holding a green glass pitcher of margaritas in one hand, two stemmed glasses with a bowl of guacamole teetering on top of them in the other, and a bag of Tostitos held in her teeth.

"What?" I said, grabbing the bag of tortilla chips from her mouth.

"I said, 'I couldn't get the door open.' So I used my elbow to ring the bell. Glad you didn't take much longer, Jax, because I was about to drop this pitcher of margs and that would have been a true tragedy."

"I've already dropped enough glass things for today. I just dropped an entire tray of beads. None of them broke, fortunately. I need that inventory for the Bead Fun sale in Portland."

Val set down the glasses on the kitchen table. "Salt?" she asked. "For the rims of the glasses?"

"Sorry, I only have table salt."

"Jax, honey, when are you going to learn how to properly stock your pantry? Really, you can't always rely on me to bring you snacks and drinks."

"It's worked for me so far," I said, shrugging.

"Here, let's open these chips, and we'll just suck the salt off them before drinking our margaritas, okay?"

"Sounds good." I admit I let Val take care of me. It makes her feel good to think she is taking care of an artist who is able to make pretty things but needs a lot of help with just about everything else— especially eating, drinking, and shopping for clothes.

I've lived next door to Val for nearly three years now, and they have been some of the best in my life. Val is enormous in every way— big red hair, pushing 6 feet tall, big bones (I say with the utmost tact), and big jewelry—the glitzier, the better. She's a hairdresser, and I am constantly surprised that any new client who comes into the salon doesn't turn and run. She's beautiful, but somewhat scary until you get to know her.

She and I live in a Craftsman bungalow in Seattle that my Great-Aunt Rita split down the middle a dozen years ago to create a duplex. I live in the right half, and Val and her series of good-for-nothing boyfriends live in the left half.

After Great-Aunt Rita died, the house became mine, and I decided to move away from the golden sunshine and giant insects of Miami.

My mom and dad still live there, and are constantly bugging me to move home before I die from mildew poisoning due to the damp weather in the beautiful Pacific Northwest. It's gorgeous here, but a different kind of beauty than Miami. In fact, it's the opposite of Miami in every way imaginable: wet, cold, rocky beaches, fewer Cubans (which unfortunately means fewer Cuban restaurants), gray skies instead of blue skies, better coffee, and better drivers.

When I moved to Seattle, I left behind more than the sunshine and my parents. I'd broken up with my boyfriend Jerry. He was more interested in watching sports, drinking a little too heavily, and eating take-out food than he was in having a meaningful relationship with me. He was upset when I left, but like he'd lost a nice watch, rather than a partner. I was not bitter. Okay, I was bitter, but only in a good, healthy way.

I'd left my job at Clorox, too. It was there I'd met Jerry, a scientific glass blower, who was the first person to show me how to work with molten glass. When my department needed a special glass part for an experiment, we would call our in-house glass blower, and he'd make a vacuum tube, or condenser, or even custom test tubes. The best part of my job was going into his workshop in the basement of the building, with its enormous lathe and the soft hum of the ventilation system. Jerry showed me it's possible to make fancy glass components for experiments, but he also taught me how to make beautiful things in the flame by melting glass. He shaped it in all sorts of ways while it was still molten: slender tubes, perfect spheres, and complex containers. Even after our relationship had fizzled, my love of glass continued burning strong.

Val and I settled down at the old oak kitchen table and filled our glasses. "What are your big plans for this weekend?" Val asked.

"I'm leaving tomorrow for a bead bazaar in Portland," I said, with probably too many chips in my mouth to be considered polite.

"Oh, that sounds like fun—or is it just bizarre?"

"Bazaar, Val, not bizarre. It's going to be terrific. It's like a flea market, you know, with people selling their beads and jewelry in booths and at tables. I'm going to stop and pick up Tessa on the way.

We're rooming together at The Red Rose Hotel where the bead sale is being held. It should be fun."

"*The* Red Rose Hotel?"

"It's the only Red Rose Hotel I'm aware of. Why?"

"It's supposed to be haunted," Val said, knitting her perfectly-plucked eyebrows. "I've heard perfume will keep ghosts away. Do you want to borrow some of mine?"

"No, Val. No. I'm sure it's not haunted." Where did Val get these ideas? I scooped up some guacamole on a chip and popped it in my mouth. Having tried some pretty terrible dishes from Val's kitchen in the past, I'm usually wary of her concoctions, but I could always count on her for excellent Mexican food. "Val, your guac is the best I've ever tasted," I said, swiping another chip through the bowl.

"Thanks, doll. I've been working really hard to become a better cook," Val said, pouring herself the last margarita. "You and Tessa are going to have fun. Maybe you'll meet a guy."

"I seriously doubt that. These shows are full of bead ladies, and even the guys are bead ladies, if you know what I mean."

"No, I definitely do not know what you mean."

"The guys who are into beads are usually frumpy. They're definitely not boyfriend material. And besides, the men are few and far between. I guess I should get into model airplanes or boxing if I want to meet some men."

"Or you could just call that hot Seattle police detective—what's his name?"

"Zachary Grant," I told her, because if I didn't, she wouldn't stop pestering me until I did, so I just skipped over the part where she pleaded with me.

"Oh, yes. Zach."

"No, apparently he doesn't like to be called Zach, only Zachary."

"He seemed okay when I called him Zach last week when he stopped by."

"What? He was here?" I was surprised the serious detective had come to see me. During the time I'd known him, he'd been stern with me and had only shown signs of kindness in my last conversation with him a few months ago.

"Oh, yes. I left you a note. Didn't you get it?"

"No, Val, I didn't."

"He said he was in the neighborhood," Val said, looking me up and down. "And Jax, you're looking good today in that V-neck T-shirt. It shows off your ta-tas."

"Thanks," I said, looking down at the front of my shirt and trying to brush off some cat hair.

"Soon you'll be asking to borrow one of my stretchy wrap around tops."

"You know I can't wear fabric like that in the studio, only natural fibers. You don't want me going up in flames, do you? You don't want polyester melting onto me like molten lava, right? But I'm glad you like the top," I said. Val had done a lot to help me embrace, or at least accept, my curviness. "In fact, you'll never guess what I found in my cleavage just a little while ago."

"I do not want to know what was in between your boobs," Val said with a grimace. She spotted the stack of bead trays and bags in the hallway. "Are you almost ready to go?"

"I've got hours of work before I leave tomorrow morning," I said, placing the pitcher and glasses in her hands. "I'll return the rest when I get back. Thanks for the drinks, guac, and chips. They were yummy. I owe you one," I said, shooing her toward the door.

"Bring me back something sparkly from the show."

"How about one of my beads?"

"Sorry, not sparkly enough," she said. "Honey, when you get back, I want you to meet my new boyfriend, Bruno."

"Sounds like a dog's name."

"Oh...yes. He is an animal, if you know what I mean," she said with a wink. "Woof!"

I didn't want to know what that meant.

"Out. Out. Don't forget to feed Gumdrop while I'm gone. And keep him away from Stanley," I said. In the last few months, we had made several adjustments in our lives after adopting a Bassett hound. My cat didn't like sharing attention with Stanley, or anything else about the dog for that matter.

"Okay, sweet cheeks, see you in a couple of days, and try to stay out of trouble. Don't forget to take some ghost-busting perfume."

I packed six full trays of my best beads, including some cute ladybugs I'd been perfecting, a bunch of earrings, some seed bead kits, and a big bag of bargain beads. With the current state of the economy, the bargain beads would probably be my biggest moneymaker. Renting the table at a bead bazaar was expensive, and the hotel room wasn't cheap either, even though Tessa and I were splitting that cost. I'd need to move some inventory to break even.

Along with beads, I had the rest of the paraphernalia needed to set up a little store for one evening and three days of sales at the bead bazaar in the hotel's ballroom: bags, wrapping material, displays, tablecloths, and lights. I tossed it all willy-nilly into the trunk of The Ladybug, my lovely red convertible VW, and sat on the trunk's lid to squish everything in. I hadn't brought much to wear, but if I wore a special necklace each day, people wouldn't notice I was wearing different combinations of the same shirts and pants all weekend long.

It was two in the morning when I fell asleep. Gumdrop, who had finally emerged from his hiding place, had snuggled up next to me. Seven o'clock arrived mercilessly early. Gently pulling back the covers, I tried not to disturb Gumdrop, who had moved to the foot of my bed. I was thankful I'd finally taught him to stop sleeping on my head. I dragged myself out of bed and walked stiff-legged and vacant-eyed into the shower, feeling like a zombie. I needed not just a cup, but a bucket of coffee this morning.

I picked up Tessa at Starbucks, near her house in Ballard. It's the coffee shop on the left side of the street at the corner of NW Market Street and 22nd Avenue NW, not the one on the opposite corner. Seattle is called the Emerald City—not because of how lush the landscape is, but because of all the green Starbucks signs everywhere you look. Tessa bought my usual for me, the biggest non-fat latte Starbucks makes—a Venti—and she had her usual single shot of espresso. I've never understood how she can function on that little caffeine in the morning.

Tessa has been my friend since we were in kindergarten, after she'd convinced me to eat a glob of paste by telling me it tasted like a mint Lifesaver. She was one of the reasons I'd decided to come to Seattle. I knew I would have at least one friend here. When I first arrived and was trying to figure out what to do with myself, Tessa invited me to her studio and there, I watched her make beads for hours. It reminded me of Jerry, and how watching him work transfixed me.

Tessa runs the local glass studio, Fremont Fire. She has an impressive classroom full of torches and often hosts classes, inviting beadmakers from all over the world to come and teach. She also sells her own earrings and necklaces as well as the work of other jewelry designers in her shop.

But Tessa wasn't selling at the Bead Fun show this weekend; she was buying. She was looking for beads and supplies that she could sell at her studio, and planning to visit with friends and see what was happening in the world of beads. Since she didn't have all her show gear, she was traveling light. She handed me my latte and tossed her bag in the back seat. I put the top down on The Ladybug, so we could take in the crisp morning air.

"Are your kids all sorted out for the next few days?" I asked between gulps of hot coffee.

"Craig promises to make sure everyone eats at least a couple of times a day, and that the kids don't play in traffic." Craig was Tessa's husband, a big huggable guy she had met when she lived in Italy. He was not Italian but an American—he'd swept her off her feet and away from Venice to Seattle, where they were now raising three kids.

They have two teenage daughters, Ashley and Izzy, who constantly fight about just everything: who gets to sit in the front seat of the van, who takes too long in the bathroom, who gets to eat the last bagel, and on and on. If that weren't enough to keep Tessa up at night, she had a surprise baby boy nearly 12 years after Izzy was born. Little Joey was a dream child, in stark comparison to Izzy and Ashley, who are difficult even on their best days.

"I'm glad to be getting out of town. The girls have been fighting like wild animals, and there are so many dirty clothes I can't see the floor of the laundry room anymore," Tessa said, settling into her seat and clipping her hair back. She was preparing for the wind that would hit us once we were speeding down the road with The Ladybug's top down.

"It's just you and me for a weekend of beads and fun."

"That's why they call it Bead Fun," Tessa agreed with a laugh, strands of her unclipped hair dancing around her face as I accelerated onto the freeway.

"No kids for you. No Val, her boyfriends, Gumdrop or Stanley for me." I was going to miss Gumdrop this weekend. Even though he was an attitudinal cat most of the time, he was my attitudinal cat and had been part of my life since I lived in Miami. He'd traveled with me across the country a few years ago, and while I did drug him to get him here, all had been fine once the two of us had settled into our new home.

"Woohoo!" we cheered as we sped down I-5 toward Oregon.

TWO

WITHOUT A DROP OF RAIN, it was an easy drive to Portland. We pulled into the parking lot of The Red Rose, an old hotel whose grandeur from a century ago had faded. The dilapidated sign out front read: *The ed ose*.

At the reception desk, I talked with a man who looked like he was pushing 80, and was in need of some serious oral hygiene.

"Room for Jacqueline O'Connell, please."

"Funny. Your name's Jackie O? Heh, heh. Jackie O. Get it?"

"I've never heard that before." Except for a million other times from old guys like him who thought they were equally clever.

We checked in and got our key card. "Good-bye, Jackie," he said as I turned to leave the desk.

"It's Jax," I grumbled to myself. It had been Jax since I was eight, when my little brother Andy hadn't been able to say "Jacqueline" and decided "Jax" was close enough. It stuck, and I've been Jax ever since. I was too much of a tomboy to be a Jackie. I like the name Jax; it has always felt like it fit me. My father refuses to call me anything but Jacqueline—he says it's the most beautiful name in the world for the most beautiful girl in the world. I have to remind him, as I leave my mid-forties behind, I am hardly a girl anymore.

"I've gotten ten texts from the girls about some new crisis," Tessa said.

"Ten messages—sounds like a crisis of epic proportion."

"It's actually twenty texts—ten from Izzy and ten from Ashley," Tessa corrected, as she walked, head down, reading the flurry of messages sent by her daughters, while juggling her overnight bag. Tessa was moving slowly, a few too many things weighing her down—including the weight of her daughters, who, I could tell, were going to make it difficult for Tessa to have fun this weekend.

We entered the elevator, and I immediately felt a chill. Tessa felt it, too.

"Wow, that's weird," I said.

"You feel it, too?" Tessa asked.

"You know, Val says this hotel is haunted."

"That's just not true. Val believes all sorts of crazy things, including that the Vulcan Mind Meld really works."

Val was an avid science fiction fan, adoring all the Star Trek TV episodes and movies. According to her, the Vulcan Mind Meld was a way of reading someone's mind by placing your hand on the temple and neck of the other person, and concentrating. She'd wanted to mind meld me before, but I always refused.

Once we arrived at the sixth floor, we hustled out of the creepy elevator and down the hall. Loaded down with gear, we tumbled into the room and took a look around. It consisted of two twin beds, with pilled acrylic floral bedspreads, two matching lamps with dented shades on the bedside stands, a mini-bar, and beige carpet that looked like it had seen a little too much action.

THREE

"I'M HEADING DOWN to set up the table for the sale," I said. Tessa didn't answer, her head down, reading the never-ending stream of texts from Izzy and Ashley. "Tessa?" Still no answer. "Bye. And don't let the ghosts get ya," I joked, poking her in the ribs as I walked by. Gathering my show gear, I headed out the door.

"Got it," Tessa said, typing frantically on her phone, and clearly not listening to my warning.

I picked up my badge from the exhibitor desk in the lobby. At the door to the ballroom, a middle-aged blond security guard with a beet-red face and a beet-sized nose to match was checking badges as vendors entered. Only vendors were allowed to enter before the bazaar started.

On the show floor, everyone was busy setting up. The convention center's ballroom was full of booths, with a different vendor at each one. Some booths were just simple tables like mine. Other sellers set up little stores with several display areas, and some booths even had mini-classrooms for impromptu demonstrations. Bead Fun was a giant sale of all things beady. People were selling all sorts of beads and jewelry: Thai silver, pressed glass beads from the Czech

Republic, tiny seed beads, African trade beads, semi-precious stones sold by importers from around the world, metal findings such as clasps, antique and collectable jewelry, buttons, chains, and, of course, handmade glass beads. If it had to do with personal adornment, someone here probably sold it. It was a bazaar in the best sense—a swirl of colors, textures, and vendors hawking their wares. I have always found these sales to be overwhelming—so much to see that I get lost and lock up from too much visual stimulation.

About the only thing you didn't have in a sale like this was street food. It was too bad someone hadn't thought to park some food trucks in front of the hotel. Food trucks in Portland were no longer "roach coaches." These days you could get almost every type of delicious cuisine from one of these mobile kitchens. Instead, we had a greasy little snack bar tucked in the back of the ballroom, its door propped open to release the smell of burnt hot dogs and day-old buns.

This was only my second show as a vendor. My first show was in the spring at Aztec Beads when I had scored a big wholesale order with one of the top designers in the country. Given the success at that sale, I was excited and a little scared about what would happen at this show. I wanted buyers to like—and buy—what I made. Great Aunt Rita's gift from beyond the grave ensured that no rent was due on the first of the month, but I still had food to buy. After all, I've been used to eating all these years, so why stop now?

And I wanted to make things I loved, so I could be satisfied with what I was doing in my life. I'd given up a lot when I left my job and moved to Seattle. I traded a forty-hour-a-week job with a regular paycheck for an artist's life that required countless hours of work with no promise of a paycheck. I reminded myself from time to time why I chose this path: to make beautiful things, to enjoy my life, and to share it with people I care about.

Walking down the aisle to my booth, I saw The Twins. They were covering their table with huge pieces of gray cheesecloth. Lara and Sara always dressed the same, and it was impossible to tell who was who. Both had long straight black hair, and they wore Doc Martens, long black skirts, and black everything else. Their designs were edgy and somber—black beads with crimson spiders, ivory skulls, and deep purple iridescent hearts with a pale white cobweb effect. I hoped to own one of their beads some day. Although I didn't think I'd ever wear one of their beads, I would love to add one to my ever-growing bead collection.

"Nice new look for the table," I told them. Both young women looked up from their work with dark, smudged eyes.

"We thought we should change up the color—get rid of the black net and get gray instead. It gives the entire montage a little more visual impact," Lara, or perhaps Sara, said in her most pretentious voice.

"Have a good show," I said, as I hurried along, to avoid hearing how no one understood their work, that they were intellectually superior to everyone in the room, and that they had been treated badly. I would probably hear it from them at some point this weekend.

I saw Indigo one row over and gave her a wave. Indigo was a beautiful black woman wearing Birkenstocks, a batik-printed skirt, and a tie-dyed T-shirt. She made gorgeous beads—sculptural leaves and flowers and glass spheres full of natural imagery. Indigo didn't believe she should actually have to sell her beads and instead, was working on a barter system in which she would simply trade her beads for food and clothing. Her biggest problem was that landlords didn't want to receive their monthly rent payment in beads—they all seemed to want cold, hard cash. For this reason, Indigo would show up at the occasional bead sale to try and make some money—and sleep in her van at night when she didn't have enough for a hotel room during a bazaar. I felt for her, knowing how hard she must have it, trying to make ends meet on an artist's income.

Next to Indigo was Vandal Beads. A man sat crossed-legged on the floor in front of the booth, sorting through show gear, which had spilled across the aisle. I had to swerve to avoid him and his chaotic mess. I was glad I wasn't going to be his neighbor for the next few days.

Down the aisle, Saundra Jameson, the self-proclaimed queen of the bead world, was talking to—no, yelling at—someone. It looked like Sal, the bead bazaar promoter who was notorious throughout the bead world as a scumbag. But he was a scumbag with a series of well-known bead bazaars across the nation that would bring in customers who were ready and willing to spend their money on beads. Saundra towered over Sal, her back curved forward as she arched over him, while he leaned backward trying to avoid cracking heads with her. I was too far away to hear what they were arguing about. Saundra shoved an envelope at Sal. He grabbed it and pushed past her without another word.

As I arrived at my booth, marked out with silver duct tape on the floor, I made a horrifying discovery: I would be at a table next to the bead diva. I was going to be neighbors with Saundra Jameson for the next three days. Oh joy.

Saundra bustled around her booth in a long crushed velvet skirt in deep purple, matching purple lace-up ankle boots, a form-fitting black sweater, and a sheer lavender scarf wrapped artfully around her neck, with a long necklace of beads hanging over the top of it. She was tall and thin, her long dark hair elegantly twisted into a chignon. Saundra certainly made me feel like I needed to review my clothing choices, which usually consisted of jeans and T-shirts. Even with Val's wardrobe help, I still had a long way to go to get to elegant.

I'd met her at Tessa's studio last April, when she'd done a bead-making demonstration. I didn't think she'd remember me from that event. I knew about her, having read magazine articles and interviews over the last few years, but I didn't feel I knew her on a personal level at all. Saundra had been making beads for about fifteen years, much longer than a relative newbie like me.

She was a walking display of her work and would stop and tell anyone she could, in exhausting detail, about each bead and where it could be purchased. Usually, she'd throw in some information about her latest show at some gallery, press a business card into the person's hand, and move on to the next adoring potential customer.

Since I had to sit next to her for the next few days, it seemed smart to start things off on the right foot. When Saundra visited Tessa's studio last spring, her giant ego had filled the room from the moment she walked in the door. Tessa told me Saundra's attitude had been surly at best. With that in mind, I thought it best to say a quick hello and then finish setting up without too much interaction.

"Hi, Saundra," I said. Saundra subtly glanced at my name tag.

"Oh, Jax, nice to see you," Saundra said a little too sweetly, as her eyes now focused on the necklace I was wearing. It was a single tubular green and pink bead I had made a few weeks ago, on a simple silver chain. She seemed to be sizing me up, seeing if I'd be any competition for her. She extended her arms as if to offer a hug. As I reluctantly approached her, she thrust her wrist in my face.

"This is the new Cosmos bead."

"Nice," I said, slowly backing out of hugging range.

"This design is one of the seven different beads you can learn to make in my new book, *Celestial Bead Designs*. No one has ever seen these designs before. I'm premiering them in this book," she said with a flourish, as she pressed a flyer into my hands.

"And as a special bonus, I've included instructions on how to make this fabulous seed bead bracelet." At that moment, the clasp on the bracelet popped open, and the bracelet slid from Saundra's wrist. I snatched it before it hit the ground. It was quite beautiful, with its labyrinthine swirls of color, set on the background of midnight blue, row upon row of tiny seed beads creating a cuff.

"Glad I caught that before it hit the floor," I said, admiring the bracelet and passing it back to her.

"Perhaps you could learn something from the book," she said. She was condescending, and I didn't like it.

"Thanks for showing me. I'll think about it," I said, quickly setting the flyer down on the side of my table.

I started setting up, first laying down a long blue satin tablecloth for the sides and front of the table, then placing a piece of black velvet on the tabletop to add a little elegance. The display furniture came out next: busts to hold necklaces, fabric-covered platforms, and tree-shaped wire stands for earrings. I pulled the lights out of their boxes and placed them on the table. Having good lighting is key to selling glass beads. Customers need to see what they are buying, and the only way they can do that is if the pieces are well-lit. I set business cards and postcards in their acrylic stands. I unloaded my calculator, receipt books, and bags necessary for sales transactions, and placed them behind my table.

I had designed the layout of my table so that the six trays of beads I'd brought would lay side-by-side in the center of the table, with stands for earrings, loose bargain beads, and kits on each end. Since I already knew where the trays would go, I would bring them down tonight before the sale started. At this point, I was about as done as I could be.

While working, I overheard Saundra talking to a slim man in his 30s with a stack of books in his arms, who had just arrived. His hair was ruffled as if he'd just fallen out of bed, and he wore a yellow thrift-store cardigan with a black and white checkered shirt buttoned all the way to the top. When I went to high school, this guy would have been the nerd who got beat up after class. In Portland today, he was something else entirely: a hipster. He was so uncool that he was cool.

Saundra wasn't exactly bossing her assistant around, but in a weird way she was coercing him, herding him, so he would do what she wanted. Anytime I heard her use the word "dear," I knew it would be followed by a demand.

"Miles, dear," commanded Saundra, "look at this mess behind the table. These cords are such a hazard, and why aren't they plugged in?"

Miles neatly placed the books he was carrying on the table beside a standing mirror. Then he scrambled behind the table to untangle the electrical cords. I watched as he plugged the lights into a black toaster-sized power box, which had been set up to provide electricity to the vendors. The units were daisy-chained together with over-sized plugs and thick cables in a line down the row, with one power box in each vendor's booth. Vendors plugged their lights, credit card machines, and any other equipment that needed electricity during the bazaar, into these boxes. At the end of each row, even thicker cables ran to a suitcase-sized distribution box. More cables snaked from this large unit up the wall at the rear of the ballroom into a utility room.

Most of the day, it was hard to miss the electrician buzzing around the room, setting up the equipment and heading to and from a utility room where I assumed the building's main power center resided. Right now he was wreaking havoc on an importer who had several tables of African tribal and trade beads. Crawling around on the floor, the electrician pulled tables this way and that, peeled long strips of black electrical tape off a roll, and wrapped them around frayed cables that were sticking out in all directions.

The importer, who according to the sign on his booth was Mr. Mboto, tried his best to remain calm during all the chaos, and was relieved when the electrician pulled himself out from under one of the tables and bolted toward the door at the back of the ballroom to turn on the power. Suddenly, the lights for Mr. Mboto's booth burst on, and I smelled burning plastic. The importer wasn't the only one with a dodgy electrical setup. The whole electrical system looked unsafe.

Miles glanced up from where he was sitting and adjusted his large tortoise-shell glasses. "Do you want me to plug in your lights too?"

"That would be great, thanks. I'm Jax, by the way."

"Miles," he said, subtly checking me out to see where I fit on the hipster spectrum. It was obvious I'd dropped off that scale years ago—if I'd ever been on it. "I guess we're going to be neighbors." Miles stood up and brushed the lint off his black skinny jeans.

"Right next door to each other here on aisle four," I said, looking down the line of tables in our row at all the other beady people setting up for the show. "Thanks for plugging in my lights."

"Miles, dear," Saundra said, looking at him, and then at me, with disdain. "You can talk to your new friend on your own time."

"I'd better get back to work here," Miles said, glancing at Saundra, who had grown quiet and was looking more intense than usual.

"We'll have time to talk this weekend, I'm sure," I said. I flipped the switch on one of my lights. No power. I was going to have to catch the electrician next time he sprinted by.

As I stood up, I ran into a woman. Actually, she ran into me. Or more specifically, she ran over my foot with her electric scooter.

"Coming through. Beep, beep," the woman said, stopping abruptly in front of me.

Wendy Wilson was a long-time beadmaker and famous for one thing: polka dots. All her beads were covered in them. She wore them along with dotted everything else: always a dotted shirt, and on occasion, dotted socks and pants. It made my eyes cross looking at all the dots swirling across her massive blouse.

"Oh. Excuse me, sorry," I said to Wendy, although I was pretty sure she was the one who should have been apologizing for running me over. "Jax O'Connell," I said.

"Jax, nice to meet you. I'm Wendy Wilson, but I suppose you already know that," she said in a self-congratulatory way.

"Yes, I do. I've seen your work everywhere. This is only my second show, so if you have any pointers, please don't hesitate to tell me."

"Be careful of people who steal your work," she said, almost to herself, as she turned back to her table and smoothed out a pile of dotted beads in a tray.

"Yes, thanks," I said. "I'll watch out for shoplifters." Thieves didn't seem like they'd be too much of a problem at a bead bazaar. But beads are small, and there are some people who might be tempted to slip a shiny trinket into a pocket if they thought they could get away with it.

I turned back to my display. Wendy's giant backside bumped into mine as she climbed off her scooter, sending me crashing into the back edge of my table. I stifled a yelp. It was going to be a challenging weekend with the bead diva on one side and the polka dot princess behind me. One claustrophobic weekend, coming up. Ugh.

As I squeezed past Wendy and her scooter in the narrow gap between the tables that led out to the aisle, I noticed Saundra's standing mirror was blocking about a foot of space at the front of my table.

"I'm going to move this mirror so it's in your space," I said.

Saundra was kneeling behind her counter and either didn't hear me, or was ignoring me. I gently moved the mirror so it was no longer blocking my table. She popped up from where she was sitting on the floor.

"What the hell do you think you're doing? You could have crushed me under there," Saundra screeched. Such a drama queen.

"I told you I was moving your mirror. It should be in front of your table, but had gotten shifted in front of mine."

"Look," she said, pointing to the ground where a duct-tape grid indicated the boundaries of each table. "My mirror was clearly within the square where the promoter wanted me," Saundra said, sliding the mirror back.

"Our squares overlap—we can't *both* be in the same spot," I said through gritted teeth.

"You don't need as much space as I do." She was waving her arms dramatically now, trying to look bigger and scarier than me.

She was succeeding. "I've got all these brochures. I have all my beads and jewelry to display. Certainly you can give up a few inches in front of your table. You probably don't have enough inventory to fill your table anyway."

I pushed her mirror until it was fully in front of her table. She was not going to bully me. "I have plenty of inventory," I said, giving her mirror a final shove.

She stood there glowering, her dark eyes fixed on me, her fists pulled up in front of her face in anger. She looked like a giant praying mantis about to rip my head off.

Time to get out of here, before I lost my head.

I grabbed my handbag and headed for the door. Everything around me was a blur of noise, color, and movement. My eyes, stinging with tears, were focused on the door. All I wanted was to get out of the chaotic ballroom.

As I neared the door to the lobby, I heard a loud crackle and watched as the overhead lights gently dimmed, brightened, and then flickered off. There was a resounding groan across the ballroom as all the vendors stopped what they were doing. Then, as quickly as the lights had gone out, they were back on, followed by a collective sigh of relief.

I was nearly run over by the harried-looking electrician as he dashed past me, a giant tool belt slung low around his scrawny hips. This was the man I'd seen earlier working at Mr. Mboto's booth. I glanced at the name tag sewn onto his untucked brown work shirt. It said *Ernie* in white cursive letters. He trotted down the aisle, past all the booths, and into the utility room. Following closely behind him was Sal, who ran the Bead Fun show. He was as sleazy as they come, propositioning any woman he saw. His pitch-black hair revealed his dependence on Clairol dye, and the paunch hanging over his too-tight belt told me he didn't get to the gym—ever.

"Why'd ya not listen to me on this? You're supposed ta have at least 100 amps in here," Sal yelled.

Ernie replied, in a thin plaintive voice, "It's not my fault. Nobody ever listens…"

I pushed hard on the panic bar—an appropriate name—on the door. What a relief to be out of the ballroom.

The lobby of The Red Rose had clearly once been elegant, but its opulence had faded years ago. Now it looked tired and worn out. Me? I was feeling the same, except for the elegant part. I don't think I've ever been that.

FOUR

I HEADED UPSTAIRS and let myself into the room. Tessa was still on her phone. She looked up briefly, waved, and continued her conversation. She had the call on speaker, and the noise erupting from her phone was deafening. Her girls were shouting at the top of their lungs, accusing each other of God-knows-what. Tessa made some false starts at trying to get them to stop, or at least to take a breath and listen. Tessa—who can be calm and cool—finally let loose her own tirade.

"Listen. Izzy. Ashley. You two are grounded and not only that, you are silenced. You may not speak to each other until tomorrow morning. You can talk to me, just not to each other. Once you both have calmed down and can act civilly, I will remove this restriction."

"Okay," said one quietly. "Okay," said the other.

"Fine. Now put Joey on the phone, so I can talk with a child who is not going to give me heartburn."

I hit the bathroom, and by the time I was out, Tessa was off the phone. Joey was a boy of few words.

"Sounds like everything is fine at home," I said with a smile.

"The girls are fighting over a boy. Izzy says she met him first. Ashley says he called her first, so she has first dibs. Now, Izzy is accusing Ashley of stealing her boyfriend," Tessa said, as she blew her hair out of her eyes, a sure sign of her frustration.

"You think telling them not to talk to each other for a few hours will do the trick?"

"Absolutely. I've just forbidden them to talk. What's more appealing than doing the one thing your mom doesn't want you to do? I expect their first topic will be how unfair it is of me to not allow them to speak to each other."

"Reverse psychology—brilliant. You have this parenting thing all figured out." And Tessa did. I wouldn't have known what to do with the girls. She knew exactly how to handle them. I'd tried to use reverse psychology on Gumdrop, but discovered he did whatever he wanted, regardless of how I tried to manipulate him.

"I'm exhausted," Tessa said.

"Me, too." I sat down on my bed opposite my friend. "And hungry."

"Then I guess it's a good thing I called room service."

"Tessa, you're my favorite person right now—and always—seriously," I said, giving her a big hug.

"How did your table set-up go?" she asked.

"Oh, I wish you had been there with me," I said. "I've got Saundra Jameson on one side, and Wendy Wilson behind me. Between the two of them, I'm going to go crazy."

"You're already half-way there."

"Very funny. Look—I'm going to need your assistance this weekend. I don't think I'll be able to deal with either of those two for long without someone to keep me sane."

"No problem, I'm good with difficult people." And that was true. Tessa had to deal with all sorts of unique personalities, to put it mildly, at her studio.

Tessa had been wonderful ever since I'd moved to Seattle. She'd taught me to make glass beads, and she brought me into her family, since my parents and my sister Connie were in Miami. My little brother Andy lived in San Francisco and worked night and day at a cyber-security start-up.

There was a knock on the door; I opened it. In the hall, a young woman in a navy smock stood stiffly with a smile plastered on her face. She heaved a metal cart into the room, pushing hard over the thick carpet. Since she was a petite woman and was having trouble managing the bulky cart, Tessa and I grabbed the handle and helped pull it along with her.

The woman whipped the silver covers off the serving trays. It was a feast of breakfast food: eggs Benedict, pancakes, bacon, melon, and orange juice.

"I think breakfast is the best comfort food," Tessa said, admiring the spread before us.

"I totally agree. My mom used to make breakfast for dinner, and I always loved it," I said, grabbing a piece of bacon and taking a bite.

"Oh, and guess what's in the minibar? Tiny bottles of alcohol. We're going to make up a new cocktail," Tessa said. She got on her knees and started searching through the minibar. "Ah. Tequila... and we'll use the 7-Up I got out of the vending machine, plus some OJ."

We each dumped a mini-bottle into a glass and added splashes of soda, orange juice, and ice.

"Cheers," we said together, clinking glasses and taking sips.

"This is terrific. With the juice, it even tastes like it should go with breakfast," I said.

"What should we call it?"

"The Portland Painkiller," I said. Tessa laughed. Hopefully, we wouldn't need too many painkillers this weekend, but so far things were not off to a good start.

"Let's eat. We'll get something in us so we can enjoy this cocktail and not pass out," she said.

The food was hot and delicious, surprising for room service, which is often on the cold side when it arrives. The meal would surely cost us a small fortune, but I didn't care. And I loved Tessa for getting this for us. I didn't have to think, or go out and find food with only an hour to go before the Preview Night.

"I wish I could just curl up on this bed in my jammies," I said. I felt wonderful—full of carbs and a little tipsy from the cocktail. It might have been two cocktails.

"Nope. Sorry. Not going to happen. Up! Up!" Tessa commanded. "Time to go downstairs, the show's going to start soon." Tessa was bossy and punctual. I am neither of those things. It's good to have a friend who can whip me into shape from time to time when I need it.

I changed into my show clothes, which could be summarized in two words: comfy and cute. I was wearing a silky black vest with a white T-shirt underneath it, and black stretchy cropped pants. Since no one would see my feet while I stood behind the table in my booth, I wore bright green high tops, and left my lime green and pink necklace on. Grabbing my rolling case of beads, I headed down to the lobby.

The Preview Night at a bead bazaar is always the best for both the sellers and the buyers. The sellers always make the most money on that night, when there's a frenzy of buyers, ready to spend-spend-spend. The opening-night buyers always want to get into the bazaar as early as possible to buy the best beads before anyone else can. Bead ladies can be a competitive bunch.

I squeezed my way past the crowd of shoppers lined up at the doors who were waiting to get inside the ballroom for the sale. The red-cheeked security guard I had seen earlier was at the ballroom door, letting in the vendors. As each vendor entered, he checked their badges, then smiled and nodded, ensuring that no customers sneaked in ahead of time. Yes, some of these shoppers would stop at nothing to get first dibs on all the best beads.

I sped to my booth. The only thing I hadn't done was to set out the six trays of beads that were in my rolling bag. Once at my table, I unzipped the bag and placed the trays on the table. Perfect. I was ready.

Saundra was fussing around with some jewelry and talking with Miles, which meant I didn't have to interact with her. The mirror we argued about earlier was no longer in front of either of our tables. Instead she had placed it between our working areas. I'd won at least one round with the bead diva, although there would probably be more arguments before the weekend was through. The mirror between us would keep her things from spilling over into my space and I hoped would minimize our interactions.

Behind me, though, it was a different story. Wendy had me squeezed in tight between her motorized scooter and her chair, which she'd pushed so far back from her table that I barely had room to move, or breathe for that matter.

At five o'clock, the security guard opened the ballroom doors, and the customers rushed in. The shoppers each had their own strategies for making the most of their shopping experience: Start at the back and move forward, clockwise, counter-clockwise; a quick jaunt through to get the lay of the land, followed by a serious shopping spree; or slowly and steadily, moving from booth to booth.

Many of the vendors would make more money on Preview Night than on the days that followed. The people who came on this first evening tended to place the largest orders and were the most knowledgeable about what they were buying. Many of them were wholesale buyers who were at the show not just to buy handmade glass beads, but also every other kind of bead from around the world.

Within minutes, the ballroom floor was packed with buyers. At some booths, shoppers were two and three deep, pressed against the front edges of the tables. It was thrilling to have people shopping at my booth. Since I wasn't a well-known beadmaker, I wasn't sure how many people would be interested in what I was selling. At Saundra's table, there was a crush of people, many of them clutching her latest book. Miles was writing up orders as fast as he could, while Saundra schmoozed with all the buyers, laughing and enjoying the attention.

Tessa stopped by my booth.

"Looks like your sales are off to a good start," she said, looking at the group of shoppers gathered around my trays.

"So far, so good," I agreed.

"I'm going to shop. That's what I'm here for, after all. Do you need anything?"

"No, I'm fine. Have fun, and let me know if you find anything you think I'd like." I loved shopping for beads, but today was not about buying, it was about selling. If I made some money this weekend, then perhaps I could splurge on something small on Sunday, and save the rest toward my next home project: a bathroom upgrade, including a glass mosaic on one wall.

I'd just finished a small update to my house, with the help of Val's sci-fi friend, Rudy, who is a house painter. Rudy did a perfect job painting my kitchen walls a beautiful shade of coral that complemented the butter-yellow color of my ancient AGA stove. He did some work on my kitchen cabinets, too, screwing the doors on properly (I had used duct tape to hold them together), and painting them in a clean, crisp white enamel. I was looking for some vintage glass drawer pulls for the cabinets to complete my kitchen, but hadn't yet found the perfect ones.

Tessa rushed off, not wanting to miss any of the wonderful jewelry that was for sale in the vast ballroom filled with aisles and aisles of treasures.

As I was starting to write up an order, the lights in the ballroom dimmed. We all paused briefly, hoping the lights weren't going to go out. Once the lights returned to a normal brightness, so did the chatter of people buying and selling. Suddenly, the room was plunged into darkness, followed by absolute silence, as we all stood still waiting for the lights to return. Dozens of cell phones blinked to life, giving some illumination to the room. The lights glowed dimly overhead for a few seconds, before the room sank back into a blackout.

Over the announcement system a thin, reedy voice said, "Ladies and gentlemen, we apologize for the inconvenience." It had to be Ernie, judging from his nearly asthmatic tone. "Please calmly head to the exits at the front of the ballroom."

At this point, everyone started moving, and chaos erupted. Vendors started scrambling to cover up their tables to protect them from anyone deciding to help themselves to some merchandise in the darkness. Arguments started between vendors and customers about whether money had changed hands during their interrupted transaction. Buyers and sellers were pushing others aside, as they tried to get to the front door ahead of everyone else. So much for Ernie's plea. People were not behaving themselves.

There was more pushing and even some screaming. Trays of beads crashed to the floor, and displays toppled. People cried in pain and surprise as they collided. There were confused conversations as buyers and sellers alike tried to find their friends in the pitch dark. I hoped everyone was going to make it out alive. I stacked my six bead trays and fumbled to find the rolling bag, but couldn't locate it. I grabbed my purse and headed toward the doors with the rest of crowd.

"Coming through, coming through," Wendy chirped, pushing her way through the crowd on her scooter. Its handlebar whacked me in the left kidney as she sped by.

The lobby was full of buyers and sellers milling around. Fortunately, whatever electrical problem was occurring inside the ballroom was isolated, and the lobby had full power. We watched expectantly through the open doors of the ballroom as the lights blinked on briefly, then flickered and went out again. The last few reluctant shoppers straggled out the door. There was no way we were getting back into the ballroom tonight.

Sure enough, the announcement came only minutes later. Ernie was at a microphone near the doors to the ballroom.

"Ladies and gentlemen. We are sorry to inform you that tonight's sales event has been cancelled due to unforeseen technical difficulties," Ernie said, trying to speak in his most authoritative voice, although he mostly sounded like he could use an inhaler.

Sal was fuming as he charged through the lobby, nearly flattening everyone in his path. He tried to grab the mic in Ernie's hand, but he was too late.

"The show will resume tomorrow morning at ten. Thank you," Ernie wheezed.

A loud groan passed through the crowd. Everyone was frustrated. I wasn't sure who was more upset—the sellers who were going to lose money by not being able to sell during what were sure to be the busiest sale hours—or the buyers, many of whom had come from miles away to "shop 'til they dropped."

Sal was screaming at Ernie about why the hotel had shut down his bead bazaar. A crowd of disgruntled vendors circled Sal, wanting to know what he was going to do to satisfy them. A group of customers stood by, gawkers watching everyone yell at one another.

I went in search of Tessa and found her at the edge of the crowd.

"Jax! Are you okay?"

"I'm fine, I grabbed my beads," I said, hoisting my stack of trays.

"Here, we can put them in my tote." She'd been hoping to fill her canvas bag with beads that she bought, not my beads. But as long as they fixed this electrical problem tonight, she'd be able to score some fun jewelry components in the next few days.

"Let's get out of here before things get ugly," I said, as I grabbed Tessa's tote and we headed toward the elevator.

FIVE

"WHAT DO YOU WANT to do now?" I asked Tessa once we were back in our room.

"Nothing. I'm tired," said Tessa, collapsing on the bed.

"And everything's okay with Izzy and Ashley?"

"They're sitting next to each other, texting back and forth. Craig said it's much quieter at home."

"I thought you said they couldn't talk to each other."

"I guess they decided there was a loophole—they couldn't talk, but they could text," Tessa said.

"Try and let Craig handle this, okay? This is your weekend to have fun. The show's called 'Bead Fun' for a reason. Let's go to the bar. I'll buy you a drink."

I was tired, but I knew where I wanted to be: in the bar—and not necessarily for the adult beverages. Although a drink would be nice, I wanted to be there to see my friends. One of the best things about bead bazaars was the chance to catch up with friends you only saw a few times a year.

"Come on, Tessa, it will perk us up," I said again, trying to convince her that staying in the room wasn't the best way to spend the evening.

"You go on without me. I'm going to take a shower, change my clothes, and then I'll head down in a little bit."

"Okay, but I better not come up here later and find you asleep in bed."

I took the elevator—it was still mysteriously chilly—down to the not-very-creatively-named *Le Bar*. It was located on the mezzanine level so patrons could look over the balcony's railing into the lobby below. The ballroom door was off to the side, locked up tight with a security guard in front of it.

In the bar, a large group sat around a low-slung mahogany cocktail table.

"Hi, everyone. Can I take this seat?" I asked, sliding into a chair next to The Twins. They seemed bubblier and less sullen than usual. Both were sipping matching nearly-neon lime green drinks.

"What have you got there?" I asked.

"Absinthe," they replied in unison. Their small hands, each finger adorned with a silver and black ring, clasped the stems of their glasses.

"Wow. I've never tried that. Is it good?"

"It is an acquired taste," they said, taking sips of the vile liquid and trying not to grimace. Clearly they had not yet learned to love it. "We understand what it's like to be tortured artists. We must suffer."

They were strange. I would never understand why they needed to be tortured artists. But I knew this: they would likely never change.

The waitress approached me. She set down a cardboard coaster and a new bowl of peanuts, and looked at me expectantly.

"You want what they're having?" she asked, nodding toward The Twins. There was no way I was drinking absinthe tonight, or any other night.

"A margarita, on the rocks, salt." It had been a day since I drank one with Val, and it was definitely time for another. The ones here at the hotel wouldn't be as good as what Val could make, but any margarita was better than none at all. At least this one would have salt on the rim of the glass, which was a good thing, since I shouldn't suck the salt off the peanuts in the bowl. There are some things I won't do in public.

"Have you seen Saundra's new book?" Minnie asked, sipping on her craft-brewed beer. Her hair was up in pigtails, and she was wearing boxy red glasses and a T-shirt with a cartoon of a baby fox on it—another hipster.

"We hate her," said Sara and Lara in unison. They were never ones to beat around the bush.

"Actually," Lara started, then Sara finished, "We hate everyone." They spoke in that annoying way old married couples often do, although The Twins were neither married nor old. They looked at each other in agreement and clinked their tiny glasses of absinthe together. I was beginning to suspect it wasn't their first.

"It's just going to make her even more unbearable. If her head gets any bigger, it's going to explode, and I'd love to be there to see that," said Lara.

"I get to spend the whole weekend standing next to her, hearing about her latest triumphs," I said, resisting the urge to bring up the altercation between us. Better to let that slide off my back.

"She's got a new assistant. Have you guys met him?" Indigo asked. Since she never had much money, I was surprised to see her at the bar, until I noticed she was drinking water.

"I saw him. Pretty cute," Minnie said, pushing her glasses up the bridge of her nose. Miles was just her type, so geeky that he was cool. At least he thought he was.

A guy I hadn't met before stopped by the bar. I'd seen him working at the table for Vandal Beads earlier. Vandal was well known for her graffiti-inspired glass beads covered with bright colors that looked like spray paint on a concrete wall. Vandal only sold her beads online, so it was a surprise to see she had a table at the show. All the images I'd seen online featured a young Asian woman in full punk gear—leather pants, motorcycle boots, a ripped T-shirt, and a spiked leather collar and bracelets—holding a can of spray paint.

"Hi, y'all here with the bead bazaar?" the man asked.

"We are! Nice to meet you. I'm Jax." Everyone else waved and smiled. "I saw you working at Vandal's booth today. Where is she?" I asked.

"Uh, look, I feel like I'm coming out of the closet by telling you this, but I'm Vandal," he replied in a hushed tone. "My real name's Vance."

"What? No way," I said. This guy looked like the Pillsbury Doughboy. No, make that the Doughboy's awkward brother. Vance was six feet tall and nearly bald, with pale skin and freckles. He wore a Hawaiian shirt tucked into jeans, and a belt just a little too high across his belly. The only thing he had going for him was that he didn't wear glasses. And at least he wasn't a hipster.

"Yep. Sorry to disappoint you," said Vance, his shoulders slumping, as he pulled his glasses out of his shirt pocket and put them on. Of course he wore glasses. Not only that, they were held together with duct tape.

"How did you get to be called Vandal? That's a really edgy name," said one of The Twins.

"I decided to call myself Vandal because it's sort of a combo of the beginning of my first and last name—Vance Dalton. Get it: Van-dal," Vance explained. "And the woman in the photos, that's my wife Lin. She's supposed to meet me at the bar."

Just over Vance's shoulder, I saw a petite Asian woman approaching. "That must be her," I said.

Vance turned and waved her over.

Lin was pretty, but looked nothing like the photos. Instead of black boots with metal studs and skintight leather, she was wearing a pale pink blouse with a Peter Pan collar, khaki trousers, and sensible black Mary Jane shoes. The only hint she was participating in the bead bazaar was the necklace of black beads with bright spray-painted designs (clearly made by Vance) that she wore as a choker around her neck.

"Everyone, this is Lin," Vance said, introducing his wife. She nodded and waved with only the tips of her fingers, standing close to Vance. "Lin, this is everyone."

As we shuffled around to make room for the couple, I noticed Luke, a charming Australian jewelry designer, sitting at the bar. He looked like he was straight from the outback with his long oilskin drover coat. A Crocodile Dundee-style hat, which he wore when he wanted to have an over-the-top Aussie vibe, was hanging from a corner of his chair back. I gave him a wave, since he was sitting by himself, inviting him to join us.

Luke was notorious for what many of us called *doing the neck* of a potential customer. That is, as he put a necklace on a woman, he'd reach up and stand close behind her and ask her to raise her hair off her neck. He'd reach around the front and lay a necklace on her, and then close the clasp. Then he'd help her put her hair back in place, giving her a little neck rub, and turn her around to admire the necklace. It worked almost every time. That man sold a lot of necklaces.

Luke stumbled over to our table. He was drunk.

"How're you mates doing?" Luke asked, trying to stand without swaying back and forth. He grabbed hold of the back of my chair to steady himself. "Hey, Jacquel—Jaz—"

"Jax," I said, so I didn't have to wait any longer for him to say my name.

"Hey, Jax. Hey, everyone else," Luke said. He flashed Minnie a well-practiced smile. "Wha's your name?"

"Minnie," she said, blushing and taking a sip of her beer.

"You come by my booth tomorrow, I set choo up with a neck nicelace, I mean nice necklace. It'll be perfect for you," Luke said, slurring his words.

"Is my good buddy Luke causing problems?" Wendy asked, shaking her head and smiling as she sped toward us on her motorized scooter. "Okay, Luke, let's call it a night."

"But I'm having show mush fun, I mean so much fun. I'm staying," Luke said.

"Come on, Luke. If you come with me now, I'll let you ride on my scooter."

"Deal," Luke said, wandering off toward the elevators with Wendy, on her scooter, herding him from behind.

Around midnight, I decided it was time to go. I had a long weekend ahead of me, and I didn't operate very well on no sleep. As I stood up, I looked over the mezzanine balcony and saw two guards standing at the door to the ballroom. One was the red-faced man I'd seen earlier checking badges. It must have been the end of a shift. At least they were keeping the place well-protected. The Twins stayed at the bar to have another round of absinthe. They'd had too much to drink and were trying to figure out how they could play beer pong without beer or ping-pong balls.

Back in our dimly-lit room, I noticed a lump in Tessa's bed. As expected, she'd never made it down to the bar.

I was feeling tipsy from my margaritas. They weren't as delicious as Val's, but they were at least as powerful. I stripped off my pants and crawled into bed, leaving my T-shirt and panties on. I was too tired to find my PJs and didn't want to rustle around too much and wake up Tessa. I had requested a 7:00 wake-up call, which was a disgustingly early hour.

When the alarm went off, I stumbled out of bed and into the shower with my eyes half-closed. Then I silently threw on some clothes. Tessa was sound asleep, the covers pulled up over her head. My friend could sleep in; she would still have plenty of time to shop for beady treasures.

SIX

I WANTED TO GET IN to the ballroom early so I'd have time to adjust and clean up anything at my table that had been disturbed during last night's blackout. There would be a giant crowd of shoppers at the doors when the bazaar opened, since no one had been able to shop for long last night. The people who weren't able to complete their sales would be looking to pick up the purchases that had been left behind when the sale was shut down.

Downstairs, I bought an extra-large coffee in the lounge and a Snickers bar from the hotel's gift shop. This was definitely not the breakfast of champions. At the ballroom entrance, there was a broad-shouldered security guard standing at the door. He was much more attractive than the ruddy-faced guard who had checked badges at the door last night. This guard was tall, with olive skin and close-cropped dark hair. He was tall, slender, and solid—like a tree. He stopped me as I tried to breeze past him.

"Sorry, ma'am," he said, with a pleasant but firm smile. "Can't let you in until eight."

"Seriously? I've got a coffee in one hand, a canvas bag full of beads in another, and my show badge hanging around my neck. You know I'm supposed to be here."

"Sorry, ma'am."

As flirtatiously as possible, I touched the corner of his name tag, so I could pull it into view.

"Rrrryan," I said, channeling my inner-Val, leaning in as provocatively as possible. "Are you sure you can't help me?" I wasn't adept at flirting, but Val had been giving me lessons. I was a poor student, especially when it came to my relationships with men.

"Sorry, I have strict instructions. I can't let anyone in until 8:00 a.m. We're trying to avoid any problems with theft."

I pulled the Snickers bar out of my handbag, peeled back the wrapper, and started eating it. "Fine. I'll just wait here and stare at you grumpily for ten minutes. And don't call me ma'am."

"Yes ma' —I mean, okay."

A couple of excruciating minutes passed, and I realized this was probably harder for me than for him. So rather than stare at him in stony silence while chewing, I decided to strike up a conversation with him. It's always nice to meet someone new, especially when he's good-looking.

I wasn't sure what my opening question should be. I certainly didn't want to talk about the weather. Conversations about the weather here in the Pacific Northwest usually went like this:

"Do you think it's going to rain?"

"Yes."

Instead, I asked, "Do you like being a security guard?"

"I like working the night shift. I come on duty at midnight and I get done every morning at 9:00 when another guard comes on duty to relieve me. I read a lot during my shift—there's not much else to do."

"What do you like to read?" I asked. I would rather talk about reading than being a security guard any day.

"The study guides for the police academy final exams."

"You want to be a cop?" Why would anyone choose law enforcement as a career? I certainly wouldn't. Of course, I played with fire for a living, so I wasn't the best judge of good career choices.

"It's better than being a rent-a-cop," he replied. And I agreed with him. If you're going to look like a cop and act like one too, you might as well be a cop. "Besides, my acting career was going nowhere."

I couldn't tell if he was serious. He sure was handsome enough to be a leading man.

"Jax O'Connell," I said, wiping any remaining chocolate from my hand before extending it. I definitely needed to read the handbook on interacting with people of the opposite sex, but Val didn't need to tell me it was not good form to shake hands when you had melted chocolate on them.

"I'm Ry—," he said. "You already know my name. Nice to meet you," Ryan said, shaking my hand and bowing slightly. Chivalry was not dead. "Looks like it's eight o'clock." And with that, Ryan opened the door to the ballroom and wished me a nice day.

"Thanks, Ryan. Catch you later," I said, lugging my bag of beads into the room.

I was the first one in the ballroom. Clearly, Ryan had done an excellent job of keeping the bad guys out. Harnessing the power of positive thinking, I was determined that this would be a successful sale. People were going to buy all my stuff. And, I was going to ignore Saundra.

I headed down the aisle toward my table. Something was wrong—my table was out of alignment. I was extra-sensitive about the location of each table, since Saundra and I had argued about it. The black velvet I had laid on the table had been pulled tight on one side, with an avalanche of earrings across it. Had I accidentally yanked my table covering when I was leaving in the dark? I hoped no one had helped themselves to items on my table during the chaos. Thankfully, my beads were in the room with me last night, but there was plenty left that could have been stolen.

Saundra's table was a complete mess, too. Her display racks were tipped on their sides, and brochures were scattered across the floor. I slipped around to the back of the tables. Beads were strewn everywhere. A silky burgundy table covering spilled off the back of Saundra's table and onto the floor. The bead diva was going to explode when she arrived. Poor Miles would receive the brunt of her anger over the messy table.

To avoid tripping on Saundra's tablecloth, I folded it over the top of her table. As I pulled back the fabric, I saw them: purple high-heeled ankle boots. Saundra had been wearing boots like this the last time I had seen her.

SEVEN

"SAUNDRA! SAUNDRA!" I yelled as I dove under the table, bringing the rest of the table covering and the contents of her table down with me. Saundra was lying flat on her back, staring upward. The mirror that had been between my table and hers was beneath her, shattered and bloody. I grabbed her hands and squeezed them.

"Saundra!" I shouted as I shook her shoulders. "Wake up!" But I knew she wasn't asleep. I pulled her onto my lap, holding her close, and checking for a pulse.

"Help!" I yelled. Someone must have come into the ballroom after I did. They could help me. No one responded.

"I'm going to give you mouth-to-mouth resuscitation now. Okay?" It seemed like I should ask for permission before clamping my lips onto someone else's.

How do I do this?

I pinched her nose shut. I took a big breath, and exhaled into her mouth. It was cold and dry. I scrambled backward. There was no chance she was still alive.

"HELP!" I screamed, hoping the security guard would hear me.

Finally, Ryan came running.

"Here!" I yelled. No matter how quickly he came, I knew there was nothing he could do to save her.

Ryan finally found us and, in an extremely manly move, picked up the table that Saundra was under and threw it out of the way.

"I haven't taken a class in CPR, so I am not authorized to perform any lifesaving techniques," Ryan said.

"I think it's too late for that," I said, out of breath.

Ryan was already on his radio, asking for help from the hotel staff.

My hands were shaking and balled into fists. My right hand was covered in blood. As I turned it over and opened my fingers, I saw a perfect round bead, glistening with blood. It was one of Saundra's beautiful Cosmos beads. And then I passed out.

● ● ●

Ryan's face was swimming in and out of view.

"Jax? Are you all right?" he said as he crouched above me. I felt like throwing up. Ryan must have moved me, since I wasn't near my table. I was lying next to the wall at the back of the ballroom with a wet paper towel on my forehead. An emergency technician was kneeling next to me, checking my pulse.

I sat bolt upright.

"You're okay," Ryan said, gently settling me more comfortably with my back against the wall for support. He removed the soggy paper towel and brushed the hair off my face.

Down the aisle from where I was sitting, a handful of cops were stringing crime scene tape around Saundra's and my tables. Tessa was talking with a surly-looking police officer. As soon as she saw me, she broke away from him.

"Jax! *Dio Mio!*" Tessa shouted as she ran toward me, stopping just short of knocking Ryan over.

One of the cops approached Ryan and called him away, and Tessa took his place at my side. The EMT continued to check my vital signs, taking hold of my arm and sliding a blood pressure cuff on it.

"What happened? Where's Saundra?" I asked a blurry Tessa, as the blood pressure cuff squeezed my arm, then released.

"The coroner's team took her away. She's dead, Jax." Tessa hugged me tight. I closed my eyes and stopped breathing while I focused on Tessa's arms around me. Those words, *she's dead*, hit me hard. Dead. I already knew Saundra had died, but hearing it said out loud made it all the more real.

"I just, I tried to save her—"

"Shhhh, there was nothing you could have done—that any of us could have done—to save her," Tessa said. She seemed so calm. Maybe that's what happens when you become a parent—you get all sorts of super-powers, like remaining calm during emergencies. With her teen girls, I'm sure she got lots of practice at being calm during a crisis.

"Excuse me," the EMT said, wedging himself between me and Tessa and removing the blood pressure cuff. "Just trying to finish up here." He took a pen light out of his kit and flashed it across my eyes. The bright light stung, and I squeezed my eyes shut. I was not a good patient. The technician must have seen enough to know I was not injured. He clicked off the light and tossed it back into his bag.

"You're not feeling dizzy?" asked the EMT.

I shook my head.

"Well then, you check out okay. If you get a headache or have any vision trouble, you get over to Providence Medical Center." He got up, grabbed his kit, and was gone in a flash.

Sal paced back and forth in front of the tables that were now ringed in yellow tape. He had to be concerned about how he was going to explain what had happened to the dozens of customers now crowded around the doors, ready to come in and shop.

"What happened to my table?" I asked.

"The police aren't going to let you into that area until they finish their investigation," Tessa said. "But Sal set up another table for you."

"Another table?"

"Sal said he had a no-show by the front door. The police won't let you take your displays or other show gear. But I've got your beads. Let's go look at the new table."

"But, why—how—can they even continue with the bazaar? That's crazy."

"I know, but Sal said the show must go on," Tessa said, shaking her head. It was outrageous that Sal would want to continue as if nothing had happened. It's not like this was *Hello Dolly*. Tessa helped me up and supported me as we walked slowly past a maintenance crew that was setting up temporary room dividers to block the gruesome scene from the view of passersby. We found my new table—my new, completely barren table.

"Tessa, can you go up to the room and get anything that's not nailed down? We're going to need to improvise a new table display."

"I'm on it," Tessa said, giving me a hug and heading toward the lobby. The surly officer, who I'd seen talking to Tessa just a few minutes before, caught up with me at my new table.

"Ms. O'Connell?"

"Jax," I said, running a hand through my hair, and trying to seem at least a little presentable.

"I'm glad to see you up and about," the officer said. "We'll need to get a statement from you, seeing as you found the deceased."

"When? Now?"

"Right now."

"I need to splash some water on my face. You want to walk with me?" The officer escorted me to the ladies' room, and I was glad he was next to me, since I was still feeling wobbly. As we walked, I told him how I'd found Saundra, and he took notes in a small black book as he listened to me recount what had happened.

"I guess this is as far as you can go," I said, arriving at the women's bathroom. I didn't think he'd follow me in, and besides, I'd told him all that I could.

"I've got all that I need for now. Thank you. You'll be hearing from one of our detectives within the next twenty-four hours so that we can collect any other pertinent information."

In the ladies' room, I stood looking in the mirror—I was pale. I splashed cold water on my face and rubbed it vigorously, trying to get the dead-person cooties off my lips. I pulled some water through my hair, too. That helped tame it and revitalize me. I took a sip of water from the tap. I felt a little better, and that was a step in the right direction.

As I was drying my hands and face with a paper towel, a whimper came from the stall behind me. I stood still and listened. Maybe it wasn't a whimper, maybe it was just my stomach growling. Then I heard it again, the tiniest, sad sound, just a few feet away. I looked down to see whose feet might belong to those pathetic sounds. No feet. What was I to surmise from this? That the person crying in the stall was a double amputee? I didn't think so.

"Hello," I said softly. "Hello? Can I help you in some way?"

The whimpering stopped.

"I know you're in there. I heard your sniffles."

Still silent.

I peeked in the gap between the stall door and its frame. Minnie was sitting on the toilet seat with her legs pulled up to her chest, her eyes red and teary. In true hipster style, she was wearing a pink checked square-dancing dress with leggings that made her look like she was eight years old.

"Minnie? What are you doing in here?"

"Hiding. I don't want anyone to see me crying."

"Oh, I know, Saundra—"

"Saundra, she's, just, uh, such a treasure. I read all her books, she was so talented, and to lose her now..."

"I know, it's hard," I said, trying to comfort her through the door. Maybe Minnie had never known anyone who had died.

"You found her. What do you think happened?" Minnie asked with a sniffle.

"She must have tripped and fallen on a cord during the blackout. I guess she cracked her head open. There was blood—"

"Right, right, right. You're right," said Minnie, hyperventilating, still inside the stall.

"Come on, Minnie, let's go. The doors will open any minute. Pretty soon this place will be filled with customers."

"Can't I just stay in here a little while longer?

"You don't want to miss out on sales, do you?"

"I just can't face people right now."

"Get your butt out of that bathroom stall before I slide under the door and pull you out. It will not be pleasant," I said with what was probably too much force. I was channeling my inner-Tessa.

And with that, poor Minnie slid the lock open, peeked out through a crack in the door, and made a dash for it.

I followed Minnie out of the ladies' room, and looked across two aisles to where my table used to be.

Passing by the room dividers that masked the crime scene, now decorated with festive posters about upcoming sales in Tucson and Santa Fe, I decided to take a peek. A piece of yellow crime scene tape was wrapped around two tables—mine and Saundra's—and there was a thin dusting of powder—fingerprint powder, I assumed—all over everything on the tables and even the floor. Saundra's body was gone. A crime scene investigator, in her white protective suit, was using tweezers to pick up bloody fragments of mirror from the concrete floor and placing them in a plastic evidence collection bag.

Sal came around the end of one of the room dividers and found me looking at the scene. He ran a hand over his unnaturally inky-black hair and looked me up and down, giving me a full body scan. A woman died on this very spot and he could still stand there looking at me lasciviously.

"You doing okay? Sorry you lost all the things in your booth, but glad you still got your beads." He was standing just a little too close. The remains of his breakfast toast still clung to his black goatee. "Oh, yeah, we found you this nice place by the front door. So don't come asking me for a refund or anything."

"Thanks, Sal." I was feeling stronger now, and ready to get to work and sell some beads. I needed to set aside what had happened and focus on work. I could fall apart later.

"You need anything, you know where to find me. If you need to rest, I got a bed in my RV out in the back parking lot, you know. I could even give you a little massage, if you wanted."

Sal was scum through and through.

EIGHT

TESSA WAS STANDING in front of my new table, giving it some final adjustments.

"You read my mind," I said, admiring the display that Tessa had created from things she had found in our room.

"What do you think?" asked Tessa.

"Is this my bedspread?" I asked, fingering the fabric covering the tabletop.

"Yes, as a matter of fact, it is," said Tessa.

"And, this is?" I asked, looking at the pretty white dish that held all my earrings.

"Stole it from our room service tray."

"And this little platform?"

"Three Gideon Bibles wrapped in a pillowcase." Tessa was proud of her creativity, standing a little taller than usual, and she wasn't that tall to begin with.

"Tessa, you're a genius. Thanks so much for this," I said, bending over the table and giving her a big kiss on the cheek. It would never be as terrific as my original table display, but it certainly looked better than an undraped plastic table with some beads lying on it.

Unfortunately, there were no lights to make everything shiny and sparkly. Unless someone miraculously had some spare lights, this was as good as it was going to get.

A grim-looking Miles shuffled toward me with a box of books. He was wearing his skinniest black jeans, a white shirt with a bolo tie, and a gray porkpie hat, another hipster fashion statement. I looked at Tessa to get some clue about why he was here.

"I told Miles he could share your table."

"The cops won't release Saundra's beads for me to sell. But I've got all these books that were in her room. She had autographed them and everything."

"Sure, Miles, you can sell them here," I said.

"Thanks, it will help with the money situation."

"What money situation?"

"Saundra hasn't paid me in a long time. I can do really well selling my handmade wood carvings and felted iPhone cases, but it's not really enough for me to live on, even in a house with three other guys. She said her money was all tied up in this book, and she'd pay me after this weekend. But now I guess I won't get paid."

"Let's try and sell the books. Maybe you can hold onto the money you make from the sales," I said. These books were, strictly speaking, not Miles's to sell, but he'd been stiffed by the now-stiff Saundra, so selling them seemed like a good way to recoup some of the money she owed him.

Miles pulled out the books, set up a few of them on the table, and sank down into the chair next to me. I felt a little wiped out, and Miles looked like how I felt. Me, from my ordeal with Saundra, and Miles, he always looked a little spacey.

"I'm going to find some food for you. It would do you both some good," said Tessa. "Coffee and a blueberry muffin for you, Jax?"

"Please." Tessa knew me so well.

"Can I bring something for you too, Miles?" Tessa asked.

"That would be nice, thanks. A gluten-free muffin and a small dirty soy chai latte."

"A what?" One of Tessa's eyes twitched—she was trying not to roll her eyes. I knew what she was thinking—Miles was a high-maintenance kind of guy.

"A muffin, no gluten."

"That's not the part I was confused about."

"I like to order things that aren't on the menu. It's a much more authentic experience that way," said Miles.

"Small. Dirty. Soy. Chai. Latte." Tessa was committing that drink to memory. I was sure she was regretting asking Miles if he wanted anything.

Tessa came back a while later and distributed breakfast snacks to Miles and me.

"You're the best," I told Tessa, giving her a big hug.

She looked over at Miles's stack of books. "How much for the books?"

"They're $25, and they have all been autographed by the now deceased author," Miles said with as much enthusiasm as he could muster.

Tessa, always on the lookout to make a profit, said, "I'll give you $200 for ten books."

"Sold," Miles said without blinking. He may have been a hipster, but he was also a capitalist.

I caught her attention with my are-you-crazy look.

"They're signed by the author, and the author is dead. Everyone knows that when an artist dies, the price of their work skyrockets. I'm buying these, and I'm going to sell them in my store for a hefty profit," Tessa said.

"Way to go, way to sell some books," I said to Miles. He tried to give me a fist bump, which I bungled by thinking it was a high-five. In the end, it looked like rock-paper-scissors. I was the paper, he was the rock.

Tessa took a copy and handed it to me. "Here's a gift for your heroic efforts."

"Thanks, Tessa, I'll treasure it always," I lied. I was really going to donate it to Goodwill so I didn't ever have to be reminded of this awful experience. I opened the cover, and sure enough, Saundra's giant spidery signature was scrawled across the inside page. I swallowed hard, knowing I couldn't look at this book today, or ever, and tossed it on the floor at my feet.

"Okay, I'm going to shop. That's why I came, after all," Tessa said.

"If you see Ryan, tell him I'd like to talk with him," I said.

"Who's Ryan?"

"He's a security guard. You can't miss him, he reminds me of a tree, but I mean, in a good way. Sort of big and solid." Today's events had seriously scrambled my brain.

"Dark green branches for hair and roots for feet?" Tessa asked with a grin, miming what branches looked like.

"About six feet tall. He's got sexy brown eyes with glints of amber," I said.

"Oh, I saw him. He looks young. I mean, younger than you—"

"Ladies, can we stop with the fantasizing about the man-tree? You're freaking me out," said Miles.

"I'm going to go drop my books up in the room, and then I've got hours of important shopping to do," Tessa said. She grabbed her stack of books, and teetering from their weight, pushed her way out of the ballroom doors.

My new table location was much better than where I'd been located originally. Even so, this was the last place I wanted to be. I wanted to be upstairs in my hotel room, or better yet, at home, indulging in what I like to call Double Bubbles—a bubble bath and a bottle of champagne. Instead, I was going to sit here and sell my beads, and try to recoup my expenses from this trip, and try not to think about dead bodies.

I had many questions from customers.

"Are these made from clay from the craft store?" "No, they're glass," I responded.

"Are these made in China?" "No, I made them myself," I answered.

"What kinds of molds do you use?" "I don't use molds, each bead is sculpted individually," I told them.

"I'll give you a buck for it." "Sorry, this is not a swap meet or a garage sale," I said, disappointed that a handmade item could be worth so little to some people.

I did it all with a smile on my face, and was glad I had the opportunity to teach people who stopped by about handmade glass beads. Mine were lampworked, sometimes called flameworked beads. I'd made each one by melting glass in a torch, and then wrapping and sculpting different colors of glass around a long thin metal rod, called a mandrel. After completing a bead, I cooled it overnight in a kiln. The next day when I removed the mandrel from the middle of the glass, a hole remained. The bead was now ready to be used in jewelry.

Minnie waved at me from across the aisle. She was about four booths down from my new location. She got up and scurried over to me, since she didn't have any customers at her booth.

"I've got to go tinkle. Can you watch my table?" Minnie asked.

"Don't forget to come back," I said, remembering that just a few hours ago, I had had a hard time extracting her from the bathroom. "Miles, why don't you go and 'man' Minnie's table," I suggested.

"You want me to go over there?"

"Seriously, Miles, if you're going to hang out with me all day, you might as well be useful." I could see why this guy had gotten on Saundra's nerves—he was not the shiniest bead on the strand. "Maybe you'll make a new friend."

Miles got up and moved to Minnie's table, taking a seat behind it. He still looked distraught over Saundra's death. He was limp—limper than usual—and his unfocused gaze seemed to be keeping customers away.

Minnie was back a few minutes later and sat down next to Miles. They talked for a little while, and he started to perk up. She pulled out her Muppets lunchbox, and he smiled with appreciation. Minnie had been looking despondent about Saundra's demise as well, but she seemed to be feeling better as she continued talking with Miles. She had a constant stream of customers at her table, not just looking, but making large purchases. Minnie helped customers make selections and wrote up receipts. Then Miles collected payments and wrapped the purchases.

Minnie made hipster beads. There was no other way to describe them. She covered all of the basic hipster motifs: owls, hedgehogs, handlebar mustaches, candy-colored skulls, and anything else that was retro, funky, cute, or odd. They were not my style, but boy oh boy, there were a lot of people out there who were crazy about her beads.

She had a lull in business around noon and scampered over to my table.

"Miles is going watch my booth while I get some lunch for us over at the snack bar. You want me to get you something, too?"

"What do they have?"

"Hot dogs and some sort of salad thing wrapped up in a tortilla. At least I think it's a salad—it's green. Whatever it is, I guess it might just be moldy."

"Geez, such great choices. I guess I'll have the hot dog." If it was cooked, maybe the micro-organisms would be dead, at least. I popped ten bucks into her hand. "And a Coke and chips, too." It was not a day to diet.

I wondered how Miles was going to be able to eat at the snack bar. There wasn't going to be much that was edible, let alone gluten-free.

"Okay, that works," Minnie said, as she headed off across the show floor, swinging her hips (maybe that's why she was a hipster), her square-dancing dress swishing side to side as she walked. Minnie strolled down the center of the aisle, waving to her friends in their booths. This was her way of saying that she wasn't going to stop and chat, or shop, because if she did, it would've taken hours for her to get to the snack bar.

After Minnie left, a woman who clearly had been shopping up a storm, judging by the number of bags in her hands, stopped by and bought one of my beads. It was a pretty bead with a bi-cone shape—a slender cylinder tapering to a point at each end. At its core, there was layer of silver foil with colorful twists of purple and aqua on the surface. This was my first sale of the day, and I realized I had no receipt books, no bags, no tissue paper, no calculator—they were all off-limits behind the crime scene tape.

"Can you wait one second?" I asked. "I need to grab some supplies."

I ran to Minnie's table. "Miles—help! I need a receipt book…Oh, and maybe a small zip-lock bag."

"No problem. I've got Minnie's supplies here. I've been processing payments for her all morning."

"Glad about that," I said, trying to hurry Miles along while my customer waited.

"Yeah, so I organized everything, since she had so many duplicates," he continued, not getting the hint that I was in a hurry.

"Whatever you have, Miles, I really need it now. I've got a customer waiting," I hissed, as I looked back at her and smiled sheepishly, holding up my index finger. Just one more minute, and I'd be right back. I thought about giving Miles a finger as well—the middle one.

"Oh, sure. Sorry. Here's an envelope of things that were duplicates. I don't think Minnie would mind if you used them," Miles said, handing me a manila envelope stuffed with papers and receipt books.

I hurried in a half-run back to my table.

"I am so, so, so sorry," I said, dumping the contents of the envelope on the table and searching through them.

"Ah, here it is. A receipt book," I said, trying to act positive and professional.

I wrote the receipt, found a small zip-lock bag, and some tissue paper. My customer was staring at me impatiently, as I hurriedly wrapped the bead. She had more shopping to do, and I was slowing her down.

"Thanks for your purchase. And thanks for your patience," I said with one final smile.

Wordlessly, the woman took her bead and vanished into the fray of people spending, spending, spending.

Minnie came by a few minutes later with lunch. "Here's your hot dog," she said, placing it on the table. "And heeeere's your mustard and ketchup packets."

What? No relish?

"Here's your Coke. And your chips," she continued, dropping them next to the hot dog. "Oh, and here's your change."

"Eighty-four cents?"

"Sorry, the snack bar is expensive."

"Thanks, Minnie. At least I won't starve." Actually, lunch wasn't bad. I put every bit of ketchup and mustard on the hot dog and that definitely helped. A few hundred calories can turn my world around.

I looked down the aisle at Minnie and Miles. They were sitting at Minnie's table, smiling and eating fries and drinking shakes. Shakes! Fries! Nobody told me those yummy options were available. And Miles—he was eating them, too. So much for his gluten-free, non-dairy existence. He was breaking all his food rules today.

I looked through the papers and supplies Miles had given me. Price tags, pens, a calculator, and a few receipt books. Among the things were a half-dozen pages with drawings of beads and notes. I shoved them back into the envelope.

By two o'clock, sales were finally picking up, and I made several large sales in the last hour that the bazaar was open. I knew I'd at least paid my expenses for the weekend. I felt good about that—even if I didn't sell anything else, I was in the black. What would my sales have been like if I wasn't using a comforter as a table covering and had an actual lighting system? I would never know. Tessa arrived a few minutes before five o'clock, when the show was about to close.

"Dinner?" Tessa asked.

"I only had a hot dog for lunch. I could use some real food."

"I'm going to meet up with Adriana and find out where we're going for dinner," Tessa said. Adriana was tall and thin with puffy white hair. She reminded me of a Q-Tip. She was a bead shop owner from San Francisco, who often came to sales to buy inventory for her store. Tessa and Adriana were old friends, although they only saw each other a few times a year at bead bazaars like this one. Adriana always knew the latest beading techniques, and Tessa loved to learn them from her.

Sal shooed the last few customers out of the ballroom. I closed the receipt book for the day, throwing a spare sheet over my table to keep it a little more secure overnight. Miles left with Minnie, only giving me a small wave as they walked out the door, eyes locked on each other, messenger bags strapped across their chests. I didn't expect to see much of Miles the rest of the weekend, since he had apparently met his dream girl.

NINE

"WHAT DID ADRIANA say about dinner?" I asked, sitting down on my bed and thinking seriously about curling up in it and missing dinner. "I can't stand the thought of going out with a big group of people. I'm still traumatized from this morning, like I have Saundra's death cooties on me."

"We can't stay in the room for another night of room service," Tessa said. "Besides, I'm feeling energized. I spent money. That always brightens my mood, at least until the VISA bill arrives. I'm around grownups and not kids who are fighting and—"

"Uh, Tessa? Let's forget about your home life for a sec," I said.

"Right. A big group of us are going to the Cheesecake Factory. Want to come?" asked Tessa.

This was not my idea of a good time, except for the dessert. Fifteen people, probably all women, crowded around a table that should only hold ten, everyone talking all at once, utter chaos when the bill arrives, and someone getting stuck paying an extra forty bucks because someone else at the table miscalculated how much they owed on the tab.

"Not going," I said.

"Suit yourself. No dessert for you then."

"What, you won't bring your best friend back a piece of chocolate cheesecake?"

"Jax, I know you're upset about Saundra, but you need to let it go. You did what you could."

I said nothing, afraid if I did, I'd start crying.

"You're just going to sit around here and think about what happened, aren't you?"

"Maybe," I said. Of course I was going to think about Saundra's death. I could think of nothing else. In fact, the idea of Saundra, now dead and cold, had haunted me all day. And I had so many questions. What had happened? Had she tripped during the blackout? Had she still been alive after we all left the ballroom, dying slowly and alone in the dark? Had she bled to death from cracking her head open on the shattered mirror?

And was this an accident, or something far worse?

"Tessa, you saw the crime scene tape and those police officers milling around behind the dividers that the hotel put up," I said.

"Wait—you're not thinking this was murder, are you?" Tessa asked. "Maybe there was something else going on, like someone stole Saundra's change fund, or some of her beads."

"Why would there have been so many police officers around if it was just a theft or an accident?"

"I can't believe it was murder. But even if it was, what are you going to do—stay here and hope that Saundra's killer doesn't come and find you here alone? Or are you going to stay here without an alibi in case someone else gets murdered?" Tessa was laying on the false concern pretty heavily now. She thought she could manipulate me. And, I admit it, she could.

"I'll go, I'll go," I said, relenting. The best way to find out if anyone else was thinking that Saundra had been murdered would be to eat dinner with a bunch of women who'd been drinking too much.

And besides, I could have a piece of chocolate cheesecake.

• • •

We took the frigid elevator down to the lobby. I was quiet as we descended, still fragile from this morning's events and uneasy with Tessa's complete denial of Saundra's demise being something more than cracking her head open. Tessa broke the silence.

"It must have been such a shock for you to have discovered Saundra. It's a huge loss to the bead world," said Tessa, crossing herself.

"I don't know if anyone from the bead world will miss her—she was pretty condescending to me and everyone else. Even you didn't like her pompous attitude when she visited your studio a few months back." In April, during a Weekend of Education, Enlightenment, and Design—we tried not to laugh when we called it WEED—Saundra had demonstrated how to make a leopard print glass bead. Tessa had had a hard time managing Saundra because she acted as if she were the star of the show, which couldn't have been further from the truth.

"She made gorgeous glass beads. She promoted the heck out of herself, and by doing that, I think she helped teach the general public about beads," said Tessa.

"Seriously, that makes her wonderful? She would never give me— or you, for that matter—the time of day. You mean *that* Saundra?" It wouldn't surprise me at all to find out that someone had killed her. People may have admired—or tolerated—her, but most disliked her as much as I did.

"But we don't speak ill of the dead," Tessa said, crossing herself again, and saying something in Italian. She could become extremely Italian and Catholic at times, and talking about death was one of them.

"Just because she's dead doesn't change who she was," I said. "I tried to save her life, but that doesn't make me suddenly believe she was a saint."

"But, Jax, someone must have loved her. She must have family members who care about her, who will miss her now that she's gone to heaven."

"Heaven? You think she'd go to heaven?"

"Yes, heaven, Jax. Don't you believe in heaven?"

"Oh for heaven's sake," I said, realizing that this was not the best response. "I just don't believe—"

"You know what, Jax? I'd think you of all people could understand that this person, although maybe not a nice person, shouldn't have died the way she did. And I believe, and I have taught my children to believe, that each of us is special, and each of us is good," said Tessa, glaring at me.

"Save your preaching for someone else—" I interrupted myself. "I'm sorry, I'm just so frazzled, I don't even know what I'm saying."

Tessa's phone started dinging, as a flurry of text messages arrived. Izzy and Ashley must have been fighting again.

"Geez, Tessa! Your phone—it's driving me crazy. Can't Craig handle the girls? Don't let all that drama at home make matters worse."

"No, Jax, *you're* driving *me* crazy," Tessa said, rummaging in her purse for her phone, finding it and gasping at what she saw on the screen. "I need to call home," Tessa said over her shoulder as she hurried away.

"I think I'll feel better if I have some dinner," I said, but what I was really thinking about was dessert and the healing powers of chocolate cheesecake. I yelled after her, hoping to lure her back. "Or maybe I'll go find Ryan. I'll bet he's on duty guarding the ballroom. No one will ever get past him. You should have seen him this morning. He wouldn't let me onto the show floor even a minute before eight o'clock. He's a real stickler, but kind of cute." She pushed through the rotating front door and was gone.

Collapsing into one of the giant vinyl chairs that lined the walls of the lobby, I dropped my head into my hands. I examined the white half-circles on the top of my Chucks and the swirls of floral carpet that headed off in all directions below my feet. If Val had seen me wearing Converse high-tops out in public, she'd have been extremely disappointed in my fashion choice, and she wouldn't have been shy about telling me. But she wasn't here, so she'd never know. Besides, they were bright green—one of my favorite colors—and not too dirty. And they were comfy.

A pair of feet appeared in my field of vision, toe to toe with me. Perfectly manicured bright pink toes. Sky-high patent leather sandals. Could it be Val, coming to haunt me because of my poor choice in footwear? That was not possible.

But it wasn't Val, just my guilty conscience playing tricks on me. I scanned the body standing in front of me. Ankles, bare knees, bare thighs, and a red mini skirt. That was followed by a skin-tight T-shirt, boobs that had possibly been surgically enhanced, a thin tasteful silver chain around her neck, and finally a face. The woman's blond hair cascaded past her shoulders. I had no idea who this was. She was clearly not a bead lady based on the fact that she was not wearing a gigantic beaded necklace.

"Are you Ms. O'Connell?" the woman said, her shiny badge flickering into my field of vision.

I jumped to my feet, a little too quickly to be graceful.

"Uh…yes," I responded eloquently. The surly police officer had told me that a detective would want to talk to me. This must be her. I needed to sit back down, but I somehow felt the need to stay standing, like a poor rookie being stared down by an army sergeant.

"I'm Detective Tiffany Houston, Portland Police Department."

Tiffany Houston was not the best name for a police detective. There wasn't much gravitas in a name like that. And she should seriously reconsider her fashion choices—she was dressed to party, not to interrogate me.

"I'm off-duty right now. Trust me when I say that this is not what I usually wear when I'm working on a case," Detective Houston said, clearly catching my head-to-toe sweep of her getup.

I nodded mutely. I was still trying to reconcile what a detective should look like with who was standing here with me. The only detective I'd ever spent any time around, Zachary Grant, always wore a suit and tie. If Val were here, she'd remind me that Zachary— or Zach, as he'd allowed her to call him—needed a consultation on choosing ties that were less ugly.

"You were involved in an incident here at the hotel?" asked Detective Houston.

"I was," I said. "Uh, detective, that incident you want to talk about, do you mean a theft? The blackout? An accident? Murd—"

"Let's have a little chat in the morning," said the detective, cutting me off. She wasn't going to tip her cards.

"Please don't discuss anything that has happened with regard to Ms. Jameson. I'll find you in the ballroom tomorrow," the detective said. With a thin smile, she handed me her card.

"Got it. See you then," I said, pocketing her card.

Turning on her shiny heel, she walked briskly through the revolving door, as Tessa had done moments before.

TEN

I PULLED OUT MY PHONE to call Tessa and apologize for being so insensitive. She was right, you shouldn't speak ill of the dead, and she was also right that it's best to avoid being alone when you've been freaked out by a dead person. In fact, Tessa is correct ninety percent of the time. Me? I'm correct the other ten percent.

I was already late for dinner. The Cheesecake Factory was only a couple of blocks away. I headed for the restaurant, leaving a message for Tessa as I trotted. Maybe I'd find her at the restaurant. And maybe I'd still be able to do some questioning of my beady friends about what they had seen in the last twenty-four hours.

The restaurant was immense. Twenty feet above my head, oversized cone-shaped art glass chandeliers hung from frescoed ceilings. Floor-to-ceiling columns covered in sparkling mosaics flanked the sides of the main dining room. The place was over-the-top—a vast gaudy cavern with dozens of tables.

I found the table where my friends were sitting. As expected, ten people were sitting hip-to-hip at a table meant for eight.

"Sorry, sorry, I'm late," I yelled, trying to get someone's attention.

They all were talking at the same time, their glass bead necklaces, earrings, and bracelets glinting in the warm glow of the brilliant chandeliers dangling like jewels above our heads.

I was happy to see Tessa sitting at the farthest end of the table. She must have been able to negotiate détente with her daughters. If she were a cartoon character, she'd have a big black cloud hovering over her head. I threw caution to the wind and headed her way. She was trapped and would have to talk with me if I slipped in next to her. She was at the foot of the table, so at least we could sit next to each other and spill into the aisle without being too uncomfortable.

I flagged down a waitress. "I'll have a Cosmo, and my friend here, I'd like to buy her a—Tessa, what are you drinking, sweetie?" I asked, trying to buy back her friendship with alcohol and cuteness. She spoke exactly one word.

"Jack."

"Yes, my dearest friend would like Jack Daniel's," I said, looking from Tessa and back to the waitress. Tessa shook her glass to make the ice cubes jingle. "On the rocks. Make it a double. My treat. Oh, and a menu, please."

The menu at the Cheesecake Factory is a short novel: twenty pages of salads, entrees, light snacks, heavy snacks, with extra pages just for desserts. I didn't look at the calorie disclosures because I knew I'd be appalled.

I scanned the table to see who else was here: Vance Dalton and his wife Lin, Miles, Minnie, The Twins, Luke the Aussie, Indigo— who must have made money today or else she wouldn't have been able to afford dinner out—and Wendy, whose scooter was parked by the front door. Miles and Minnie were a few chairs down from us, making goo-goo eyes at each other. Ah, hipsters in love, it was enough to make me lose my appetite. I was going to have to ignore them to make it through the meal.

Tessa hadn't warmed up to me yet. The waitress arrived with her new drink. Hopefully, my friend's mood would improve soon. I smiled at her as she took a sip of her drink, trying to say non-verbally,

"Who's your best friend?" She gave me a small smile, but that was all. The waitress took my order, chicken piccata, and dashed off. I hoped my food would arrive as quickly as Tessa's drink had. I was starving.

"How was the first day of the bazaar for you?" I asked Vance, who was across from me.

"Disappointing. It felt like people were looking for Vandal, and all they got was me—not the most exciting guy."

"Your work is fascinating, though. People should be judging you by what you make." As we sat there, Vance adjusted the duct tape on the temple of his glasses. There were some things he could do to improve his appearance. If Val were here, she'd insist he needed an entire make-over, starting with a new pair of glasses. Whether that simple fix would improve his sales remained to be seen.

"I'm going to go back to selling on the Internet. There aren't as many people to interact with in person that way," Vance said.

I noticed Vance's wife, Lin, hadn't said a word, but seemed entranced by The Twins, who were wearing their usual black on black dresses. Sara and Lara were unhappy, more unhappy than usual.

"What's up, you two?" I asked.

"We hate this bazaar," one of them said. "There are never enough customers who are into our work, you know?" said the other one. "No one is deep enough to understand what we do," said the first one. "I'm so glad we aren't sell-outs like Saundra was." They both nodded in agreement, looking at each other, and then back at me.

"What about not speaking ill of the dead?" I asked, trying to redeem myself with Tessa.

"We have no problem with death, especially when it's someone we hate," said Lara, or possibly Sara.

"But you two hate everyone," I replied.

"So?" they said in unison. "We hated her for more reasons than—" said Sara, possibly Lara. "Shut up," whispered the other one, as quietly as possible. This was the first time I'd ever seen any tension between these two. It made me wonder, though: Did one—or both— of them hate Saundra enough to kill her? And if not The Twins, could there be someone else who disliked Saundra enough to want her dead?

"Did you two see anything strange last night during the blackout, or after?" I asked.

"No," said one of the women. "It was dark, and after that, they wouldn't let us back into the ballroom."

"We love the dark. It's what we live for—and death, of course."

"Yeah, that one hipster chick down there, she was freaking out during the blackout," said the other.

"We hate her," said the first one.

"What's wrong with her?" I asked.

"She totally co-opted our skulls," they said, showing more emotion than I'd ever seen from them, each clutching the stem of her glass so tightly that their knuckles were turning white.

"What did she do to your skulls?" I asked, trying to figure out if *co-opted our skulls* was code for brainwashing.

"You know we make these skull beads, and they have been our trademark for a really, really, really long time," said one, as the other bobbed her head in agreement. "That hipster chick, she totally started making them, too."

"It's so derivative. I mean, we were making skulls for a couple of years, and she comes along and makes skulls, too."

"Maybe they look different than yours."

"They do," said one, "and they are hideous—"

"They are all these cute colors—"

"Not the colors that true skulls are," said the first.

"There you have it—she uses different colors. They're not like yours at all, are they?" I said, trying to convince them that it's common for artists to make similar designs, but that doesn't mean a design has been stolen.

The Twins said nothing, but sat there staring at me. As if on cue, they both took a sip of a vile bright yellowish green concoction. They were drinking absinthe again. Drinking a Cosmo suddenly seemed much more interesting than talking with these two dimwitted Goth chicks.

I was feeling a little woozy, but it couldn't have been the Cosmo, since I'd only had a sip of it. The day's events must have been catching up with me. I looked around the table. Could anyone here hate Saundra enough to want to kill her? It was temping to grill each one of them, to ask where they were when the lights went out. Did anyone have a reason to kill Saundra? Could I have their fingerprints? And a little DNA? I admit those last couple of questions wouldn't get me far. I also knew I'd promised Detective Houston that I wouldn't discuss what had happened—whatever that was—with anyone.

And that made me wonder: Why had a detective come to see me? Was that the normal procedure when someone finds a body? When I'd found a dead body a few months back, it was clear that the woman had been murdered. But this time, I couldn't be certain if it was murder. It may simply have been an accident.

I noticed Miles staring off into space at the other end of the table. Was he upset that Saundra was dead? He seemed like a nice guy, maybe a little too nice, given how badly Saundra had treated him. He was generous enough to have lent me some supplies when I needed them today. Although those supplies were actually Minnie's.

I called down the table to Minnie, "I think I have some extra papers of yours, if you're looking for them."

Minnie looked up from her drink, a fancy cocktail with sprigs of herbs sticking out of it. It was the same thing that Miles was drinking. She seemed surprised, her round brown eyes getting rounder in response to my comment. Minnie nodded. The restaurant was loud, and it was hard to tell if she heard me. In fact, the restaurant was getting louder and louder, though I wondered if that was really true, or if I was just becoming overly sensitive to everything after the trauma of the morning.

"I saw you had a lot of duplicate receipt books and other supplies, so I lent some to Jax, since the cops took all of hers," Miles told Minnie.

"You're going to come back and help me with my booth again tomorrow?" I asked Miles.

Miles's shoulders dropped, disappointed that I wanted him back. "Yes," he said, sighing. "I'll be there tomorrow to help." One of his hands was under the table and so was one of Minnie's. No doubt they were holding hands.

My chicken dinner arrived, and it was large enough to feed a small village. I was sick inside, and not because of the crowded table and the din of the restaurant. I was overwhelmed. I'd never experienced a day like today. While I had seen a dead body before, I had never held one in my arms and looked into blank eyes, never tried to resuscitate someone—and failed. I tried to concentrate on my breathing, but as I did I started to shake, my chest hitching each time I inhaled. I grabbed two twenties out of my handbag, threw them on the table, and bolted for the door. I needed to breathe, to walk, and to cry.

ELEVEN

I WALKED AS QUICKLY as I could, dodging waiters and customers as I left the restaurant. I passed the dessert display case without so much as a glance. Any other time, I would have stopped, or at least slowed down, to admire the decadent cheesecakes: salted caramel, chocolate mousse, white chocolate raspberry, and a dozen more.

I flew out the door and headed away from our hotel, or maybe I was headed toward our hotel. I was never very good with directions. A familiar voice called out me—it was Tessa.

"Hey! Jax! Wait up."

I kept walking. Moving through the cool evening air helped me clear my head. After three blocks, I stopped at a corner, doubled over in pain, sweaty and out of breath. Tessa caught up to me. I felt her familiar touch as she put her hand on my back.

"Time to slow down, my friend. You're not running a race," she said, gently rubbing my back.

We started walking again and after a few blocks in silence, I finally said, "All I can think about is Saundra. I can't erase the memory of her. The blood on her head, her eyes, still open—how cold she felt in my arms."

"She must've been dead for hours," Tessa said. "I'm sure the coroner will figure all that out."

"I just wonder...Why is she in the morgue?"

"Because that's where dead people belong. I don't think Miles would have the wherewithal to prop her up in her booth, *Weekend with Bernie*-style."

"That's not what I mean. What if someone wanted her dead?" I asked.

"Who would want her dead—" Tessa started to ask, but we already knew the answer.

"Don't get mad, I'm not speaking ill of the dead. I'm just talking facts. I can't think of a single person who liked her."

"But that doesn't mean someone would want to kill her. Jax, I know you've had some success with finding murderers. You figured out who killed Misty at the bead shop, and that was amazing," Tessa said. "You're upset, but don't let what happened this morning, or what happened months ago, lead you to obsess about someone's dark motives."

"I know. The world doesn't work that way. People die, but it doesn't mean it's murder," I said, but still, I wondered what had really happened. "A detective came by after you left. She wanted to talk with me about Saundra."

"I think that's normal. It doesn't mean someone killed her. It's just standard operating procedure."

I pulled Tiffany's card out of my pocket. I hadn't looked at it when she gave it to me.

Tiffany Houston
Portland Police Bureau
Homicide Detective

TWELVE

"HOMICIDE?" TESSA SAID, stopping dead in her tracks.

"I think homicide detectives usually investigate murders, not the theft of beads and jewelry."

"Or accidents—if there had been something suspicious that needs to be investigated. It could still be an accident, the police just need to verify that."

We finished our walk to the hotel in silence. After I'd bolted from the restaurant, I had no idea where I was. Tessa guided us effortlessly back to The Red Rose Hotel. She was clearly a better navigator than me.

I didn't feel like passing out, and I felt steadier on my feet. And I was glad Tessa was talking to me again.

• • •

Back inside the hotel, we headed toward the elevators. The door to the ballroom was open.

"Tessa—let's take a peek inside," I said.

"Let's just leave things alone. It's none of our business."

"It feels like my business. Especially since that detective wants to interrogate me tomorrow morning," I said. "It would be nice to have as much information as possible before I talk with her."

"Why? You don't need to know anything. Just talk with the detective and tell her what happened. You don't have to go looking for extra details."

"Please, Tessa. Look, you didn't clamp your lips on a dead woman's mouth this morning. You didn't find one of her glass beads in your hand and faint. You didn't—"

"You just want to talk with that hot security guard. I'm going up to the room."

"Okay, okay. I promise I won't be long. He's a security guard. At least I know I'll be safe."

"Be careful, Jax. You shouldn't get mixed up in this mess and put yourself in danger. Remember last time, you nearly got yourself blown up—"

"I'll be careful, I promise," I said, turning her around and giving her a gentle nudge toward the elevator.

Slowly craning my neck, I peeked around the edge of the ballroom door. Ryan turned the corner at the entrance to the ballroom and crashed into me. I fell backward, landing on my butt, with Ryan standing over me. He offered me his hand, and I pulled myself up as gracefully as possible, finding myself just a little too close to him once I was standing. Oh my, his eyes were beautiful—dark brown with little flecks of amber. I decided those colors were my new favorites and couldn't wait to get back to the studio where I could experiment melting glass in those delicious chocolate and caramel hues.

"Hi, Ryan, what a surprise running into you," I said, dusting myself off and stepping back to a more comfortable distance. "What are you doing here?" What a silly question, he was doing his job.

"CSI finished up their evidence collection, and they've asked me to secure the perimeter."

"Can you tell me anything—do they have any information about what happened?"

"That's on a need-to-know basis," he said.

"Come on, Ryan. Tell me what's going on."

"Look, I shouldn't be telling you anything—but then again, there isn't much to tell. These CSI guys, they've dusted for prints and taken all sorts of things away with them. They say it's going to take weeks to get the results of the fingerprint tests. This isn't like television, where the detectives get the test results in twenty minutes."

"I knew that. Pshhh. It's not like I believe all the things that happen on those crime shows. Are they just going to pack things up, go back to the office, and hope they get some results someday?"

"I'm afraid so. I'm hoping I can do my part with the homicide investigation. That might help me get a good job after I graduate from the police academy."

"Aha! So it was murder!" I said, a little too loudly.

"Shh. You're not supposed to know that. As far as you or anyone else at the bead bazaar is concerned, Saundra's death was just an accident. The woman fell, cracked her head open, and bled to death."

"Maybe I could help you figure out what happened," I suggested. "This needs to be settled fast, before everyone leaves the bazaar on Sunday and heads home. Once everyone's gone, it'll be harder to figure out what happened."

"I'm working with the police on the case. You don't need to worry about it, especially after all you've been through," Ryan said, as he offered me a chair and sat down next to me. He leaned toward me. "Are you feeling okay? That must have been quite a shock."

"I'm okay, feeling better. Thanks for helping me this morning."

"Oh, all part of the services I offer," he said with a warm smile.

I cleared my throat. "Yes, well. I—"

"You must be upset that Ms. Jameson died," he said.

"Saundra was pretty condescending and rude. It sounds terrible, but she was obnoxious." Then, remembering that Tessa had warned me about speaking ill of the dead, I added, "But she must have some family members who care about her."

"You do realize, Jax, that you're the number-one suspect?"

"What? Me? Because my table was next to hers? Because I'm the one who found her? I'm not a killer," I said, shocked he would think that of me.

"That's what all murderers say," Ryan joked.

At least I hoped he was joking. Some of the people I'd seen at dinner strolled by on their way to their rooms.

"Do you have an alibi for last night?" he asked.

"Yes. I was in bed. Tessa was with me. I mean, we were in the same room, each in a bed, together, in the same room."

"That's good," he said, leaning closer. "I wouldn't want to have to turn you over to the police."

"Me neither."

"Who do you think would have a reason to kill Ms. Jameson?"

"No one. Or, everyone, depending on what you consider a valid reason to want someone dead," I replied. "She wasn't the nicest person, but so awful that someone would kill her? I don't know."

"That narrows it down considerably," he said, shaking his head.

"I'll keep my eyes open and tell you if I hear anything suspicious. That is, if I see, or hear, anything…" I wasn't making much sense. Definitely time for bed.

"I need to get back to securing the facility. Good night, Jax. I hope I see you again…soon." If Ryan had had a hat on, he would have tipped it.

"Good night," I said.

Oh, I love a man in a uniform.

The elevator felt chilly again tonight, but that was a relief, since I felt warm around the edges from talking with Ryan.

• • •

"You were gone an awfully long time for someone who was just going to stop and say hi to that security guard," Tessa said, with teasing accusation.

"Oh, but Tessa, he's so, you know—"

"Good-looking?"

"And you know how I like tall men—"

"No, no, no," said Tessa, grabbing my shoulders. She sat me down on the bed so she could look me in the eyes. "We will have none of that falling in love at first sight thing happening here. This weekend is complex enough without you mooning after some guy. Got it?" She was right. We'd only been in Portland for a day, and things were already more complicated than I'd ever imagined.

"Got it," I replied. Tessa was bossy, but in a good way. She kept me out of trouble. Sometimes. "I had a good talk with Ryan. Apparently, I'm a murder suspect."

"Wow, you were right all along. It is a murder," Tessa said, shaking her head in astonishment.

"Good thing you were here with me. I have an alibi," I said. "No one can accuse me of killing Saundra. You can vouch for me."

Tessa didn't say anything.

"Right?" I asked.

There was an awkward silence growing between us.

"Right?" I asked again.

"I wasn't in our room last night," Tessa blurted out.

"What? Yes, you were. I saw a big Tessa-sized lump in your bed."

"That was all my clothes in a big heap. When I got to the room, I pulled everything out of the suitcase while looking for my beading supplies. It was such a big mess, I flung the bedspread over the top so you didn't have to look at it."

"If you weren't in our room, then where were you?"

"Adriana called and said she'd show me how to make a bracelet with seed beads. I went to her room, we played with beads, drank some wine, watched some bad television, and I fell asleep. When I got back to the room in the morning, you were gone, so I just let it slide."

"So that means neither of us has an alibi."

"I was in Adriana's room all night, so I have an alibi. But you were here all by yourself," Tessa said.

"And it also means I just lied to Ryan about my alibi," I said, "and when he finds out, he'll think I'm—"

"*Colpevole*," Tessa said, her Italian bubbling up as she realized she was the reason I had no alibi.

"English, Tessa—in English, please."

"Guilty."

THIRTEEN

WE SAT ON OUR BEDS facing each other.

"Someone killed Saundra. And it wasn't me," I said. "But we have to find out who did."

"No, Jax. We don't have to do anything. We're going to go to bed. I'm exhausted. For once, you're not going to be the one to solve all the problems in the world."

"And you know, just because the police think it was a murder doesn't mean it actually is a murder. The investigation could turn up nothing. What do you think?" I asked.

Tessa didn't answer. She had fallen over onto her pillow, fast asleep.

It was my bedtime as well. I called the front desk and requested a seven o'clock wakeup call. I wanted time to get up and do some snooping around in the morning before the bead bazaar opened, and hoped that if I could at least clear my name as a possible killer, I'd have a much better time this weekend—to say the least. I didn't want to be dragged off to jail on suspicion of murder.

If I could make it through the weekend, I could get home and go back to a normal life. A simple life with Gumdrop, and Stanley the basset hound bouncing back and forth between my house and Val's. I wanted to be at home with Val next door bringing me food from time to time and reminding me that life was meant to be fun and lived to the fullest. But while I wanted to be back home, I couldn't leave without knowing who had killed Saundra. There was a killer among us. Could that person kill again?

My comforter was downstairs on my sales table, so I dragged the spare blanket out of the closet and wrapped it around me. I stared at the dark ceiling and thought about what had happened today. What had the medical examiner seen that would compel the police to open a murder investigation? I fell asleep, still thinking of the buyers and sellers at the bead bazaar. Who could be so cold-hearted as to want to take another person's life? Who could be more cold-hearted than Saundra herself?

I dreamt of darkness with flashes of glimmering lights. After each illumination, I searched in vain before being plunged back into an impenetrable black void. Nothing. I couldn't see a thing. I was scrambling in the dark.

I woke to the sound of the phone ringing. Gah! Seven o'clock came far too quickly. I reached over and picked up the phone, expecting to hear the pre-recorded voice: "This is your seven o'clock wakeup call." Instead, I heard nothing. "Hello? Hello?"

"Stop it. Or you're next," whispered a croaky voice.

"What? What?" I shouted into the receiver. "Who's there?" I heard a click. Whoever it was had hung up the phone.

Tessa, from under her pillow, said, "Wrong number?"

"No. It was someone threatening me, telling me to stop it. I don't know what that means. Stop *what*?"

"Who do you think it was? Someone at the front desk? Maybe they know you like to steal the little shampoos in the bathroom, and they're calling to tell you to stop it?" Tessa said, sitting up in bed.

"Someone's trying to frighten me," I said. And they were doing a really good job at it.

"Seriously? Now you truly have lost your mind. It was probably just a crank call. Izzy and Ashley used to make calls like that, until they realized that caller ID showed their names to whomever they were calling. That took the thrill out of it."

"Maybe it was Saundra's murderer," I said.

"You said it yourself—it might not even be a murder. No murder, no murderer."

I looked at the red numbers glowing on the clock on the bedside stand. It was 5:30 in the morning and I was wide awake. There was absolutely no need for a wake-up call.

"I'm going back to bed," said Tessa. She crashed onto her side once again, pulling the blankets over her head. Tufts of dark brown hair stuck out from under the covers. At least I knew she was in bed last night and not off who-knows-where.

I changed my top and slid on some shoes as quietly as I could, but that probably wasn't necessary. I think a full brass band could have marched through our room, and Tessa would still be sound asleep. If I was going to be awake so early in the morning, I was going to have to find coffee immediately. Fortunately, there was a Starbucks across the street. Just like in Seattle, there are several Starbucks in every large American city, including Portland. I would be disgusted by this if it weren't for the fact that I loved and needed coffee every day, and especially now. I bought two scones, a latte for myself, and an espresso for Tessa. Even if the espresso was cold by the time she woke up, I knew she'd drink it. Like me, she just can't resist caffeinated beverages.

I entered the lobby and passed by the ballroom entrance. Ryan was sitting in a folding chair reading, where I had left him hours ago. As soon as he saw me, he stood up—such a gentleman. "What are you doing up at this hour?"

"I couldn't sleep. Too many bad dreams." I wasn't sure yet if I wanted to tell him about my scary phone call.

I sat down next to him. I was wearing my PJ bottoms, but I didn't care. Take me or leave me—this is how I looked this morning. Along with my flannel pants, I was wearing a classy long-sleeved T-shirt from New Orleans. "Show Me the Beads" was written across my chest in purple sparkly letters. At least I was wearing a bra. In case Ryan had some beads to throw at me, I wouldn't be revealing too much when I flashed him, as women do during Mardi Gras. I would never show someone my ta-tas for a strand of beads, but there were some bead ladies who would.

"Espresso? Scone?" Poor Tessa was going to have to fend for herself for breakfast. I hoped Ryan liked espresso because there was no way he was getting my latte. Ryan took one of the brown paper bags with a scone in it in one hand, and the tiny espresso cup in the other. Actually, the cup wasn't that small, it was that he had nice, big, manly hands.

He took a sip of the espresso and winced. "How much sugar did you put in this?" he asked.

"Three packets. Tessa likes her coffee extra sweet."

"Maybe I'll just eat one of the scones," Ryan said, putting the cup back into the cardboard tray and removing the crumbling pastry from its bag.

We sat there quietly for a few minutes. I decided I'd tell him about the phone call.

"I got a scary call this morning. Someone threatening me," I said.

"What did they say?"

"They told me to *stop it*—but I don't know what *it* is."

Detective Houston told me not to talk with anyone about Saundra, but Ryan was involved in the investigation, too. He wasn't just anyone, and besides, it wasn't like I was trying to corroborate my story with someone. I was just having a conversation with a hotel security guard. A hunky, sweet-natured security guard.

Ryan sat there chewing and thinking. It looked like he was puzzling through the timing of the events on the night Saundra died.

"I went on duty at midnight and was stationed here all night. I'm certain no one went in or out during my shift, so whoever killed that woman didn't enter or exit during that time."

"That's for sure, you're strict. You certainly didn't let me in until exactly eight o'clock yesterday morning," I said, teasing him.

"I completed my security check at the start of the shift, then sat and read, as usual," Ryan said.

"Security check?" I asked.

"At the beginning and end of each shift, the security staff checks the exterior exits to confirm that they're locked. And we spot-check the stairwells to ensure that we don't have any undesirables hanging out in them."

"Oh, yes, scary people who find dead bodies, or are killers, who—"

"I wasn't joking when I asked about your alibi last night. You're a suspect."

"What? No. Not possible."

"I overheard some of the vendors mention they saw you talking with Saundra earlier that day and that you two were having a disagreement. Since your booth was next to hers, the police must think you had the best opportunity to kill her without being seen," Ryan said.

"We were fighting about our booths, but I wasn't pissed off enough to kill her." Now, I really was pissed off and wished Saundra wasn't dead, so I could kill her. She had no right to go and die and make me look like a suspect. I hoped I wasn't saying those words out loud.

"Did you see Saundra during the blackout?" Ryan asked.

"The ballroom was dark. I couldn't see anything," I said.

"You didn't see Saundra after the bazaar shut down?"

"I don't remember seeing her in the lobby. It was chaotic out there. Tessa and I didn't stick around long," I said.

"It's a good thing you have an alibi for that night."

"I have something to tell you about my alibi."

FOURTEEN

"TESSA WASN'T WITH ME that night. She was in a friend's room playing with beads. So I don't actually have an alibi. Sorry, but I swear I wasn't out creeping around killing people." I started to tear up, realizing as I said it that having no one to vouch for me that night would mean even more police scrutiny.

"I don't really think it's you," he said, handing me a napkin to wipe my tears. I sniffed a little and then pulled myself together. Hoping it wouldn't leave a foamy milk mustache, I took a big gulp of latte.

"Think about the people you know. Any ideas about who would want to kill this woman?" Ryan asked.

"I don't have a clue. No, actually I know lots of people who would want her dead, but no one who would actually kill her." I knew I hadn't killed her, but other than that, I really didn't know where to start. "I met a detective last night. She wants to talk with me today. Do you know her? Tiffany—"

"Houston? I've met her. She's new on the force, just moved up from Los Angeles. Apparently it's her first time working in Homicide. She's been assigned to this case."

"I'll let you know how it goes with her," I said. "Well, I'm exhausted, and I've got a whole day ahead of me. I've got to get ready for it."

Taking the coffees and my remaining scone with me, I lifted my tired body out of the chair. Ryan rose with me, and touching my hand, said, "Take care of yourself, okay?"

I nodded, looking up at his kind face and internally sighed. At least, I hope I hadn't sighed out loud.

The elevator doors were just starting to close. I made a dash for it and slipped in. I nodded a greeting to the woman already in the elevator and pushed the button for my floor. When the doors opened, the other passenger turned right toward the even-numbered rooms, and I went left toward the odd-numbered rooms.

I reached for the key card in my pocket and realized I didn't have it, only the credit card I'd used at the coffee shop.

"Tessa," I whispered through the door, hoping not to wake up the entire hall. "Tessa!" No answer. I knocked a little bit. No answer. I pounded a little louder. "TESSA!" I was half-shouting now. I didn't want to stand in the hall for hours while Tessa slept.

The door was ripped open, but instead of the irritated yet groggy Tessa I expected to see, Miles stared out at me.

"Miles?" I shrieked. "Miles! Why are you in my room?" He looked small and pale with just a sheer scarf wrapped around his waist. I tried not to look down, not wanting to see any more of Miles than was absolutely necessary.

"Uh, look, this isn't your room, okay? It's Saundra's. I didn't want to go back to my house where my roommates party all night. I thought I could sleep here instead, since she wasn't using it any-more, why—why—let it go to waste?"

"Saundra's room." It was more a question than a statement. Where was I? I looked at the door number next to Miles's head: 511. I had a sudden realization: My room was 611. I had gotten off on the wrong floor and was now interrupting whatever it was that Miles was doing. What was Miles doing? I peered over his shoul-der and saw a mortified-looking Minnie sitting up in bed with only a sheet covering her, staring back at me like a deer caught in the headlights.

"Well, I, uh, guess I'll be going. I'm sorry to have interrupted, I mean, sorry to have startled you. Really sorry—it was an honest mistake, all these hallways look alike."

"Crap, Miles, haven't you ever heard of a peephole? I swear—" Minnie hissed. I didn't get to hear the rest of her rant, as the door clicked shut. I slunk away. Three minutes later I was at room 611, banging on the door and yelling at Tessa to let me in.

When she finally opened the door, I nearly knocked her in the forehead.

"You are never going to guess what's happening exactly one floor below us."

FIFTEEN

"YOU KNOW WHAT THIS MEANS?" I said, as I broke my scone in half and passed it to Tessa.

"It means you should really keep track of what floor you're on before you start pounding on doors?"

"Yes, that, but it also means we know which room is Saundra's. And her room may hold a clue to who wanted her dead, because it certainly wasn't me. It means I'm going to have to get back into Saundra's room later and investigate," I said.

"I don't want you to do that," Tessa cautioned. "If you get caught, you'll be moved to the top of the list of suspects. You'll look like you're trying to cover your tracks."

"According to Ryan, I'm already at the top of the suspect list," I said. "As long as I don't get caught, any clues I find can help us figure out who the killer really is."

"Jax, think about it. I'm certain the police would have swept everything up and out of Saundra's room by now. You're not going to find anything there."

"But Miles had a fancy scarf wrapped around his waist when he answered the door. It looked like one of Saundra's."

"The police didn't clear out her room?"

"It didn't look like it."

"Sounds like shoddy police work to me," Tessa said, heading to the bathroom to get ready for the day. "But, not our problem, right?"

It may have not been Tessa's problem, but it certainly was mine.

• • •

My first customer of the day was a woman with short brown hair, artfully spiked on top.

"Let me know if I can answer any questions," I said to her. She was wearing a choker of seed beads woven together to create an intricate pattern. Seed beads are tiny, some nearly as small as a grain of sand. Bead designers stitch and weave those tiny beads together, mixing tones and shades to create elaborate works of wearable art. At the center of her necklace was a beautiful emerald-colored scarab cabochon, a flat oval with a beetle design. Small seed beads in all shades of green delicately encircled the cabochon. The piece was stunning.

"Nice beads. I love the ladybugs," the woman said, picking up a handful to examine them. "These are adorable. I'll take them." She pulled every single one out of the tray. "I've been making necklaces like the one I'm wearing for friends. But I've had many requests for necklaces for little girls. I'm thinking a smaller version of the necklace with a little ladybug in the middle would be cute."

"What a terrific idea. Let me get these wrapped up for you," I said, taking the beads from her. I found some tissue and baggies among the supplies that Miles had given me.

"Once you make the necklaces, please send me a picture. I'd love to see them," I said as we completed her purchase. "And I can do wholesale pricing if you decide you'd like to purchase a larger quantity."

"Good job, Jax," Tessa said when the spiky-haired customer had left. "You've not only broken even, I think you're making a profit at this bazaar."

At least something was going well this weekend.

• • •

"Hi, Ms. O'Connell. Let's chat now," said Detective Houston as she approached my table. She looked startlingly different than when I had seen her last night. Today she had on a crisp white button-down blouse, only a conservative number of buttons undone, and a serious navy skirt. She looked respectable.

"Tessa, can you stay and watch my booth while I talk with the detective?"

Tessa sighed and blew her hair out of her eyes. "Don't take too long, I'm missing valuable shopping time."

"I'll hurry back, I promise."

As we crossed the lobby, the detective's cell phone rang. "Sorry, I need to take this call," she said, taking a few quick steps to get ahead of me so I wouldn't hear her conversation. I kept pace, hoping to eavesdrop and learn what, if any, progress had been made in the murder investigation.

"The victim's room wasn't sealed? Get up there and do it. Now," the detective said, keeping her voice low. Without saying good-bye, she hung up. Then she brought me into a conference room, closed the door, and sat down across from me.

"Ms. O'Connell, so nice to see you again," she said, reaching across the table to shake my hand.

"Yes, nice to see you, too, Detective Houston." But the truth was she was the last person I wanted to see.

"Please call me Tiffany. Oh, and I'm sorry you had to see me looking like that last night," she said. "Ms. O'Connell—"

"And you can call me Jax."

"Did your parents really name you that?"

"My real name is Jacqueline."

I watched as she typed my name into her iPad. She looked up and smiled. She was different from the other detective I'd met earlier this year. Detective Zachary Grant had been more than a little testy during a murder investigation at Aztec Beads. But after that case had wrapped up, he definitely seemed like a much kinder guy. And cute, in that Clark Kent sort of way.

"Let's see. My first question. Did you kill Saundra Jameson?" Tiffany looked at me, her head cocked, waiting for my answer.

What? This is not how these interviews are supposed to go, are they?

"No."

"Hmmm. Do you know who did?"

"No." Seriously, where did this woman learn her interrogation skills?

"Can you tell me who might have wanted to kill Ms. Jameson? I need to make a list of individuals to chat with."

Chat? Is that what this is? A chat?

"Miles, who was Saundra's assistant. You might want to check him out," I said.

"Why do you think he would kill Ms. Jameson?"

"She didn't treat him well. But Miles killing Saundra doesn't make a lot of sense because he worked for her. Without Saundra, Miles is unemployed."

Tiffany was furiously taking notes on her iPad. Since when did police departments have enough money to supply their staff with state-of-the-art computer hardware?

Tiffany saw me eyeing her iPad. "We got them in a drug seizure. After the case was closed, no one claimed them, so the department found a use for them," she said defensively and got back to business.

"There were hundreds of people at the sale the night Ms. Jameson died. Might one of them have had some issues with her?" Tiffany asked.

"Most of us who were selling at the bead bazaar knew Saundra, and most of us didn't like her. But seriously, bead people aren't known for their violence," I said.

"Jax, unfortunately, you're one of the suspects, and at the top of my list."

"And why is that?" I asked defiantly.

"You were seen arguing with the deceased. That's a motive. Your booth was located next to Ms. Jameson's, and there was a black-out—giving you the opportunity to kill her. And the means to kill

her—well, I'm not at liberty to discuss how she died. We'll be looking into her assistant's background and motives as well," she said,
looking up at me, more serious now. "I want you to help me. Got it?
You're going to be my eyes and ears here at the bazaar."

"Uh—" I said, being particularly eloquent at that moment.

"And you know why you're going to help me?" she continued without waiting for an answer. "Because if you don't cooperate, I'll be taking
you down to the station and booking you on suspicion of murder."

"Me?" I couldn't believe what I was hearing.

"You. My helper. Isn't it terrific to be on a team?"

I thought it was great to be on a team when it was voluntary. I
didn't really like the idea of being forced to help Tiffany.

"I don't think—" I started.

"You don't want your friends to see you cuffed and escorted by
me and two uniformed police officers through the bead swap meet."

"Bead bazaar."

"I'm glad you agree that you don't want that to happen," Tiffany
said without waiting for me to capitulate. "Now, who would have a
list of all the vendors and buyers who are participating in this event?"

I was officially on Team Tiffany. Ugh.

"Sal, the sale's producer, he'd know all of the vendors, and any
registered wholesale buyers. But he wouldn't have the names of the
retail buyers and hobbyists who showed up for the sale without
registering."

"I'd like to chat with him. Do you know where I can find him?"

"Sure, I can introduce you to Sal."

We exited through the back door of the hotel into a large parking
lot. Sal's small dingy RV sat on the far side of the lot.

Note to self: Do not become a bead bazaar promoter because you
will have to live like this.

Off to the side of the lot was Indigo's Ford minivan. A small
cooler and a folding chair were sitting next to the front wheel, which
likely meant she was camping this weekend.

"Hello?" I called tentatively through the crack in Sal's open door.
I slowly pushed the door open. "Sal?"

He was facing away from me, sitting at the table in his tiny kitchen. He jumped up and looked at me, startled. His eyes looked more bloodshot than ever.

"Hi, Sal."

"Do you need to lie down?" he asked, nodding his head encouragingly, ushering me in.

"Sal, this is Detective Tiffany Houston. She's investigating Saundra Jameson's murder," I said as she squeezed herself into the room behind me. There was definitely not room for three people in here. "She needs to talk with you."

"I'm not talking to nobody without my lawyer," Sal said. How did this guy own and run a successful company with grammar like that?

"Why don't you call your lawyer?" Tiffany asked.

"I don't got one." He crossed his arms and squinted at us.

"Thank you, Jax. I'll take it from here," Tiffany said.

"You're welcome. No problem," I said. She had dismissed me. Closing the door behind me, I dropped down the RV's three steps to the parking lot pavement. I'd left Sal trapped inside with the detective. Or, was it that the detective was trapped inside with Sal? Now that I'd shut the door, I knew there was no way I could eavesdrop, so I started back to the hotel.

I heard the door to the RV swing open. I stopped in my tracks.

"Yo! Jax! Can you come back in here for a little minute?" Sal asked. "The detective here, she wants to ask me some questions, and you know, last time I was alone with a cop, it didn't go so well. Like I got accused of some things that maybe I did, maybe I didn't do."

Detective Houston stood behind Sal in the doorway of the RV. Gritting her teeth, the detective said, "Yes, Jax, if you wouldn't mind joining us, that would be nice." The long hiss at the end of the word *nice* told me otherwise. She was unhappy that I was joining them in the RV, just about as unhappy as I was. I had not escaped.

I reluctantly mounted the steps of the RV and squeezed myself into a banquet seat across from Sal. The detective did the same.

"Listen, Mr…" Tiffany said, prompting him for a last name.

"Salvatore."

"Okay. Sal Salvatore." She said the words out loud as she typed them into her iPad.

"No, really, my first name is Bernard. I hated that name, it wasn't a good tough name. Plus, the initials were B.S. So I made all the guys call me Sal back when I was growing up."

"Look, Mr. Salvatore." Tiffany's voice was taut with impatience. "All I need to do is ask a few simple questions. It won't take long, and it will help with my investigation."

"Okay, shoot. Well, well, well, not really, of course," Sal stammered.

"I'm a detective. We tend to just talk to people, not shoot them," she said, trying to reassure Sal that she wasn't the shooting type. "What is your relationship to Saundra Jameson?" She was speaking more quickly now, trying to get on with the interview and out of the room. It was muggy and with Sal's less than perfect personal hygiene, the smell was approaching vile.

"She was one of the vendors at my Bead Fun bazaars," Sal said, trying to act casual, but not doing a good job of it. "She'd rent a booth a couple times a year and teach some classes."

"Anything else you'd like to add?" asked Tiffany, leaning closer to Sal, and then, thinking better of it, leaning back again in her seat. We sat there quietly for a few minutes, Tiffany idly tapping a fingernail on the table. Sal had more to say, but needed some encouragement. He was trying to be a tough guy, but clearly something was bothering him.

"Hey, Sal, listen. If you know something that will help us…" I said.

"Look, I might as well say it, because if you do some snooping around, one of those nosey bead ladies is gonna tell ya," Sal said, rubbing yesterday's five-o'clock stubble. "She pissed off some students, always lookin' down her nose at everyone, telling them their work is a piece of crap. One time in Los Angeles, she just didn't bother to show up to teach a class. Just sayin' —"

"She had a way of pissing off a lot of people," I said, but decided it wouldn't be prudent to add that I'd been one of the people she had angered recently.

"Can you get me a list of Saundra's students? Are any of those students here this weekend?" asked Tiffany.

"Yeah, there's one guy who's here who was really angry. He came all the way from Sydney for the class in L.A. This guy, Luke, he was plenty pissed off from losing all that money flying out."

Now that was interesting. Luke from Australia. Would he be angry enough to kill Saundra because he'd lost at least a thousand dollars when she was a no-show? And the night of the blackout, the night Saundra died, he'd been drinking and was blitzed in the bar. Maybe getting drunk was his way of dealing with guilt after killing someone.

"I'll need a list of all the vendors at this event, plus any other buyers you're aware of," the detective said.

"Yeah, yeah, I got that here somewhere..." Sal pushed aside a plastic keychain shaped like a giant bead that had the words Bead Fun pasted across it, a grubby cell phone, and some crumpled gum wrappers. He picked up a stack of papers.

"Oh, just one more thing. Do you have an address for Ms. Jameson?" asked Tiffany. "We've been attempting to contact her next of kin, and the phone number we've been calling has not been answered. I thought I'd send an officer out to the property. She's local, isn't she?"

"She told me once she lived somewhere out in the country near here with a brother. That's probably who you're trying to reach." He flipped through the stack of papers in his hands and found the page he was looking for. "Here's her contract," Sal said, shoving it across the table. "You can have it. I don't got a use for it now."

I glimpsed Saundra's address on the contract before Tiffany folded it into the cover of her iPad. That information might come in handy.

"And where were you during the Preview Night?" Tiffany asked Sal.

There was a pause long enough to drive a freight train through. Sal was looking straight at us, actually just above our heads so that he didn't have to make eye contact, arms still crossed. He wasn't talking any more.

Tiffany stood up abruptly and moved around the table toward Sal. As she moved past him, she snapped a business card next to his elbow on the table.

"We'll just have to bring Mr. Salvatore downtown to do a more thorough interview," she said.

Once we were out in the parking lot, Tiffany said, "Thanks for your help, Jax. We have some valuable new information that may help us find the killer."

"But I'm wondering if this really is a murder. I mean, couldn't Saundra have fallen and whacked her head?"

"Oh, Jax, you'll just have to trust me on that one," she said as we crossed the tarmac. "Now, that assistant of Ms. Jameson's—where can I find him?"

The detective and I crossed the lobby and went back into the ballroom, where the bazaar was in full swing. Tessa was finishing up a sale as we arrived at my table.

"That's Miles over there," I said, pointing toward Minnie's table, where he stood taking a credit card from a customer. "Do you want me—"

She cut me off.

"No, Jax. You've been quite helpful enough, for now. No packing up early and heading home. I'm sure I'll need you again," she said, diving into the crowd of bead-obsessed shoppers.

"You're assisting the detective?" Tessa asked.

"She sort of strong-armed me into helping her. The sooner she finds the killer, the better. She'll be off my back, and I can get back to what I'm here to do—sell some beads."

"Well, I've sold quite a few while you've been gone."

I peeked in the cash box. "Excellent job."

The detective escorted Miles toward the lobby. He looked like he was going to throw up and was as pale as when I'd seen him standing in the doorway of Saundra's room. As he passed my table, he dropped his messenger bag behind it. Without making eye contact with me—too embarrassed, no doubt, from me catching him so exposed—he asked, "Watch my bag for me?" He kept walking with the detective close behind him, without waiting for my response.

They were, no doubt, headed to the conference room to have a little chat.

I was quiet for a while. I knew what I wanted to do. I just didn't know how to broach the subject with Tessa.

"I don't like it when you're this quiet. It almost always means you're scheming." Tessa gave me her most indulgent smile. "You're going to Saundra's room, aren't you?"

"I heard the detective say that Saundra's room hadn't been sealed yesterday and ordered an officer to clear out her things and seal it," I said. "I've got to get in there before it's too late—before everything's gone. And we know Miles and Minnie aren't in there right now." It was probably not the best idea to go snooping around Saundra's room. My stealth skills were terrible. Ryan had slammed into me the night before when I was trying to be sneaky. Though, I had to admit, that had turned out all right.

I liked Ryan and wanted to help him. He seemed like my kind of guy—easy to talk with and kind. His broad shoulders and warm smile made me like him even more. If I could learn something about Saundra and what had happened to her, it might help Ryan with the investigation. And beyond that, it would be great if he didn't think I was a murderer.

"You better be back here in fifteen minutes, or else."

"Or else what?" I asked.

"Or else I'm calling the cops!"

"You're not going to do that, Tessa, you love me too much," I said, heading out the door.

• • •

Armed with the key card to Saundra's room, which I'd easily located in Miles's messenger bag, I slowly climbed the stairs, hoping to slide in the side door undetected. I had a stitch in my side by the time I got to the fifth floor and promised myself I'd start doing more cardio when I got home. I crept out the stairwell door. Several room doors were open, and a yellow housekeeping cart was at my end of the hall. A Spanish-language radio station was playing, and the vacuum roared in lucky room 513, nearest the stairway. I needed to pass by that room to get to room 511. This wasn't going to be easy.

Just like Wile E. Coyote carrying around a bush as his own portable camouflage while stalking the Roadrunner, I was going to use the maid's cart and roll it along past the open door where the housekeeper was Hoovering. She was probably so far inside the room that she wouldn't see the towel cart rolling by, as if guided by mysterious forces. She probably wouldn't remember where she left the cart and become suspicious when she found it in a new location. She probably wouldn't even care if she found me in the room. Probably.

I crouched down behind the cart and started rolling it down the hall, the cart shielding me from the door of 513. As I duck-walked beside the cart, I hoped no one would open another door. Not only would they be astonished to find a middle-aged (well, pre-middle-aged) woman hiding in the hallway behind a stack of towels on wheels, but they'd scare the crap out of me. The cart's wheels made a *squee-squee-squee* sound as I sidled along. Fortunately, you couldn't hear anything above the sound of the radio and the vacuum. When I finally reached my destination—it was only about twenty feet, but it felt like a mile—I slipped around the end of the cart. Room 511 had been sealed with crime scene tape. Dammit! I was too late. The police had already been here. I tried to figure out how hard it would be to peel off the tape, gently tugging at a corner of it. This was not a good plan. I needed to get out of there before anyone saw me trying to break in.

The hallway was quiet. The silence was deafening. The vacuum was off and the radio was, too. As I slowly turned, I saw the maid, hands on her hips, her black hair pulled into a tight bun, her eyebrows pulled into a single V above her dark beady eyes.

I gave her my most winning smile, the one my mom always told me I should use when I wanted to make new friends.

"Hola," I said, as confidently as possible.

She ripped into me with the fastest and most aggressive Spanish I'd ever heard. I'd been caught. And my Spanish was basic at best—even with three years of high school Spanish and my whole life in

Miami, about all I could do was order margaritas. Which sounded pretty good right now.

I raised my hands in surrender, but mostly to show her I wasn't holding anything. She glowered at me. We were in a stand-off, and she wasn't moving until... what, I didn't know.

Lowering my hands, I pulled Miles's key card out of my pocket.

"See, I'm okay. I'm a guest at this hotel. Here's my key." I hoped she understood what I was saying because there was no way I could manage to say it in Spanish. "I was confused and came to the wrong room," I fibbed and flashed another smile. She wasn't buying it.

She pointed toward the elevator and shouted a single English word. "Go!"

I walked as quickly as possible to the elevator door, trying to be speedy but also nonchalant, in that *I didn't just try and break into a crime scene* way. I hoped the maid wasn't going to call security, because I wasn't looking forward to explaining this escapade to Ryan or one of the other security guards.

SIXTEEN

BACK IN THE LOBBY, I dropped into a slick vinyl chair, glad I'd escaped from that catastrophe. Once again, I found myself looking down at my Chucks. They rested on fancy carpeting that looked like it could use a good steam cleaning, or better yet, replacement—some of the stains looked like they might never come out.

For the second time this weekend, a shiny pair of high-heeled sandals entered my field of vision. Oh geez. Tiffany had finished her chat with Miles and was back to make her next demand. The feet in front of me had the same pink toenails I'd seen last night. Earlier, when we were together, I hadn't noticed Tiffany's feet. With the rest of her practical clothes, she must have felt she could let loose a little with cute sandals.

I followed the legs up. These were not Tiffany's legs, skirt, blouse, or face. I nearly fell over.

"Val?"

"Bruno, he came over, and I was with Rudy—"

"Val, what are you doing here?" I asked.

"Bruno was so angry, I thought he was going to punch Rudy, even though he and I are just friends!"

"Val, what are you doing here?" I asked again.

"I slammed the door in Bruno's face and got out of town—"

"Val, who's taking care of Stanley?" I hoped that asking a different question might derail her from the frantic telling of her story.

"I dropped him off at Tessa's. I just had to get out of there."

Craig had his hands full with the kids, without adding a high-maintenance dog to the mix. I hoped Tessa's house would still be standing when we got back on Monday.

"And Gumdrop? Where's Gumdrop?" I asked.

"Do you know if they allow pets at this hotel?"

"Do not tell me you brought Gumdrop with you."

"Okay, I won't tell you."

An oversized neon pink tote was sitting at Val's feet. It had a strange boxy shape. I knelt down and listened. A deep purr vibrated from inside the bag.

"You brought Gumdrop with you?"

"I couldn't leave him at home. He'd get lonely."

"Actually, Val, Gumdrop doesn't understand about lonely. He really wouldn't have cared. In fact, he might have been glad to have all of us out of his house for a while." Gumdrop thought of the house as his own, and that I was merely his servant, feeding him twice a day, and supplying him with the occasional cube of frozen catnip.

"I was worried about him, and I didn't want to leave him at home in case Bruno came back."

"How did you manage to drive down here without going insane from Gummie's howling?" The cat and I had driven from Miami to Seattle a few years ago. For the first couple of hours, all he did was howl, "Yelloooo. Yelllllloooo. YeLLOOO." I finally had to drug him with a kitty Ambien before I lost my mind.

"I gave him a double dose of catnip," Val told me. "Can a cat overdose on catnip? Because he seemed pretty limp after the second cube." Gumdrop was addicted to the tiny catnip-infused ice cubes that I make for him. I wished I'd never introduced him to the stuff. He had become a little drug addict.

"I don't know, Val, but he's alive, because I can hear him purring. Next time, though, only one cube at a time."

"Oh, and the other thing is that I played him some classical music on the ride down, and he seemed to really like that."

"Classical?" I'd never thought to try that.

"Oh yes, he especially liked Taco Bell's 'Canon in D,'" Val said.

"Do you mean Pachelbel's 'Canon in D?'"

"It made me so hungry we had to stop for tacos."

Time to change directions here before Val had anything more to say about classical music and Mexican food.

"We'd better get out of the lobby before someone realizes you're smuggling a cat. And before Gummie comes out of his catnip-daze and starts yowling," I said.

Val grabbed her giant pink tote with my cat inside. I walked her toward the elevator. She looked nervous.

"Jax, you know that thing I said about this hotel? You know about the g-h-o-s-t-s," Val said. I couldn't understand why she felt she needed to spell, because if any ghosts were listening, it's likely they'd know how to spell.

"I haven't seen a single ghost," I said, reassuring her. I realized she didn't know about Saundra. "Look, Val, I'm going to need your help. We've had a murder—"

"Oh honey, you didn't kill someone, did you?" asked Val.

"No. Seriously, Val, concentrate."

"What can I do to help?" asked Val.

I gave Val the Readers' Digest version of the weekend's events. "Here's my key card for room 611. Go on up, let Gumdrop out of the tote, and put the Do Not Disturb sign on the door," I said. "Tessa and I are sharing a room. We'll get a roll-away bed for you. There will be plenty of space. Did you bring anything other than Gumdrop?"

"Oh, yes, I've got an overnight bag in my car for occasions such as these."

"Occasions in which a deranged boyfriend causes you to flee your house with a neighbor's cat to come to a bead bazaar?"

"In general, any emergency situation."

"Val, I'm going to have trouble doing much snooping around because all of the vendors already know me and Tessa. But they don't know you."

"Got it. You want me to interrogate everyone."

"No. No, I don't want that."

Val looked at me with a pout, her glossy bottom lip sticking out.

"What I want you to do is go shopping." Val seemed to perk up immediately. "I want you to go through the ballroom and shop at several of the booths to see if you can overhear anything the other vendors have to say about Saundra, or anything that seems suspicious."

"I can do that," she said, leaning in with a conspiratorial grin.

"Take Gummie up to the room and then come back down and get started. Here's a map," I said, grabbing a brochure with a layout of the booths. "I'm circling all of the vendors that I want you to visit."

"I can do this. You can count on me, honey."

"And make sure it looks like you and I have never met."

"Got it," Val said, giving me a little salute and nearly poking herself in the eye with her long red thumbnail.

"Wear this necklace, so you look like just another bead lady," I said, taking off my choker, a beautiful piece made with three large beads of clear glass with purple and sparkling gold aventurine swirls.

"Oh, sparkly, I like it," Val said.

The elevator arrived, and Val stepped in, lugging the enormous tote with my cat inside.

"Why is it so chilly in this elevator?" Val asked as the doors started to close. "Do you think it's poltergeists?"

The doors closed before I could answer. I didn't think it was poltergeists.

SEVENTEEN

TESSA WAS PACING BACK and forth behind my table when I skidded to a stop in front of it.

"Why did you take so long? What happened?"

I told Tessa all about my failed attempt to enter Saundra's room. As I was about to tell her about Val, I noticed that she was staring wide-eyed at a voluptuous redhead entering the bead bazaar.

"That looks just like—" Tessa said.

"Val? Yes, that's because it is Val."

"What? What is Val doing here? She's not a bead lady."

"She is today. There was a crisis at home. She's apparently staying for the weekend. I asked her to do some snooping around. Everyone knows us, or at least they know me, because I'm the one who found the body."

"Who's watching Stanley?" Tessa asked.

"He's staying with a friend," I said vaguely, deciding I didn't need to tell her that the minimally-potty-trained dog had been added to the chaos at her house this weekend.

"And Gumdrop, where is he?"

It was going to be harder to avoid answering this question.

"He's, um, he's…"

"Do not tell me. Just do not tell me she brought your cat with her."

"Okay, I won't tell you," I said. "Just be careful when you open the door to the room, so he doesn't escape."

"*Che casino*," she muttered.

Tessa used the phrase a lot around me. It meant "What a disaster" in Italian. She often switched into her native language during times of stress or when she was drunk. I'm sure she wished she'd been drinking. I had a feeling that would happen tonight.

I filled Tessa in on my conversations with Tiffany and Sal.

"Listen to this—Sal said Luke lost a lot of money on non-refundable airline tickets when Saundra was a no-show at a class in Southern California," I said. "And, of course, he said that Saundra was rude to her students—including Luke. That could make him angry enough to do something rash." We looked across the ballroom and watched Luke as he adjusted a necklace around a petite blonde, her face flushed with excitement—or was that embarrassment?—from all the attention Luke was lavishing on her. Luke was well-known, or perhaps a better word was notorious, for being a ladies' man. He was rugged and tan, and looked like he spent more time in the outback than in a studio designing necklaces. With his lovely Aussie accent, no one—well, no woman—was immune to his charms. He laid it on especially thick when selling in his booth. He'd put a necklace on me once, and I swear, I needed a cold shower after that.

"He seems like he's more of a lover than a fighter—or killer," I said.

"But what about Sal? Isn't he also a suspect?" Tessa asked.

"I guess so. Anyone who was here on Preview Night could be a suspect."

"Not just that, Jax, think about it. Luke wasn't the only one who lost money when Saundra didn't show up for class," Tessa said.

"That's right, Sal would have had to refund money to all the people who had planned to attend," I said. "That could be thousands of dollars."

"And he wouldn't have gotten a refund on any of the classroom space he rented."

"Okay, so Luke's on the suspect list, plus Sal," I said. Both men seemed shady enough to do some unsavory things, but I couldn't believe murder was one of them.

EIGHTEEN

TESSA HAD RETURNED from her latest shopping spree with a bag of books about everything from beadmaking to macramé, and dumped it under my table.

"Whew!" she said, taking a seat next to me. "I'm going to have to stop for a while and rest."

"Hi, ladies," said Val in a whisper as she arrived at my table, trying to look like a casual shopper. She looked around cautiously, to see if anyone was watching.

"Having fun?" I asked.

"I'm not going to stand here long. I don't want anyone to get suspicious of us," said Val. "I can give you a full report later tonight."

"Are you done shopping?" Tessa asked.

"Yes. I'm all burned-out on beads. I mean, really, don't you get tired of looking at beads?"

"No," we responded in unison.

"I mean, really, when do you finally have enough beads?"

"Never," Tessa and I responded. We needed Bead-o-holics Anonymous.

"Seriously?" Val said. "I've got to do something else. I can't look at another bead."

"What are you going to do then?" I asked.

"I heard there's a fun place called the Saturday Market. It's supposed to have arts and crafts and artisanal food. You *know* how I love to eat yummy things. And I heard it can be a real hot spot for singles."

"Val—wait. We'll be done at five, so meet us back in the room and we'll go have dinner," Tessa said.

"Okay, ladies. Sounds good. Unless I get a better offer. I better go now, before anyone gets suspicious," Val said as she gave us a discreet wave and swished out the door.

"I'm going to check out that sale on Thai silver beads," Tessa said. "Anything I can get for you?"

"No, I've at least a pound of those at home."

"See you back in the room," Tessa said, before making a beeline for the table on the opposite side of the ballroom.

Adriana approached my table. Today she was wearing all white with a long cascading necklace of Swarovski crystals. Val would have exactly two things to say about the outfit: That it was too far past Labor Day to be wearing white and that the necklace Adriana was wearing was her favorite piece of jewelry because of how sparkly it was.

"How's the sale going for you?" Adriana said, picking up a handful of bargain beads and rattling them like dice. She seemed nervous.

"It's going well, all things considered," I replied.

"Oh yes, I heard the terrible news about Sandy, I mean Saundra. Back in the old days before she became a big deal, that was what we all called her." Now this was interesting news. Adriana knew Saundra, and had known her for a long time.

"I hope you'll be joining us for karaoke tonight at Club Arigato," Adriana said.

"I'm not much of a singer." Not a singer *at all*.

"Oh, none of us are. It's just our chance to have fun. Don't make us come and drag you there," Adriana said with finality. In her mind the matter was settled: I was going out tonight.

I had just been Shanghaied to a Japanese—not a Chinese—restaurant.

• • •

My phone rang while I was sitting behind my sales table. I answered it.

"Jax. Hi. It's Zachary Grant. I'm glad I reached you."

Detective Grant, the prickly Seattle detective I'd met a few months before, was calling me. How strange.

"Hi," I said, trying to find some words that would make sense right now.

"I suppose you're wondering why I'm calling. I was driving by your house—"

"Driving by? Just happened to be in the neighborhood?" I asked. I wondered how often Zachary drove by. Val had said he'd stopped by looking for me last week. Curious.

"Ahem." Zachary cleared his throat. He sounded nervous. "Yes, well, I thought I'd stop by. You're not home, are you?"

"No, I'm in Portland this weekend."

"That's good because there is a burly man standing on your front steps. He looks angry, like he's waiting for someone."

Bruno. Val was not exaggerating, as she often did, about her crazy boyfriends. Bruno must have been looking for Val. I was glad she was safe with me. Safe, except for the murderer who was lurking around the hotel somewhere.

"Oh yes, I know who that is. He threatened my neighbor Val and her friend Rudy."

"Do you want me to send some officers over to move him along?"

"I think that would be good. Thanks."

"And Jax, do you mind if I stop by some other time?" Zachary asked, with a warmth I'd not expected to hear.

"Sure, I'd like that," I said. The stern detective might not be as prickly as I thought.

• • •

The bazaar finally closed for the day. I grabbed my handbag and Tessa's sack of books, and headed for the lobby. When I got to the elevator, Vance was waiting for it. "After you," said Vance, holding the door open for me.

"Thanks," I said, as the doors clunked shut.

"Sorry your table display got taken away," Vance said.

"Tessa and I came up with some creative solutions for making my booth look presentable. I just wish I had some lights."

"Hey, you know, I have some lights you can use."

"That would be amazing, thanks."

"Let's get off at my floor, and I'll get them for you."

When Vance opened the door to his room and I saw what was inside, my heart stopped. He—and Lin—were kinky. Very kinky.

His print advertisements were always over the top—his wife dressed in outrageous garb—but what he had stored in his room was much more extreme than anything I'd ever seen in any of his magazine ads. Vance and Lin were into bondage, discipline, and whatever SM stands for in BDSM. I wasn't familiar with all the ways people could punish each other in the bedroom, but they seemed to have covered all the bases.

"Vance?" I said, standing in the open door, unsure if I wanted to enter what looked like a torture chamber. I stared around the room, full of all sorts of kinky accouterments: leather cuffs with rings, high heeled thigh-high boots, a whip, a cattle prod, and red satin ropes. It was too much for me, especially the cattle prod.

He noticed my hesitation. "Oh, don't worry, it's nothing. It's just some props for our next photo shoot," he said, rummaging around in a black crate on the floor. "Here they are."

I took a few hesitant steps into the room, leaving the door open. Vance handed me two adjustable photography lamps. They would work fine as impromptu lights for my displays.

"I'd better get going," I said. This room was giving me the creeps, and I didn't want to stay a moment longer than I needed to. "Thanks for the lights; they'll help brighten things up at the new table."

"Can you stay a while?" he asked as he headed for the door. Was he going to block me from leaving?

"No, I—uh, I told Tessa I'd meet her back up in our room. I don't want her to worry about me," I said, struggling to hold two lamps, my purse, and Tessa's heavy bag.

"Do you want me to drop the lights off at your booth in the morning?" Vance asked, noticing that I was about to drop everything I was juggling.

"That would be terrific. Thanks." I slipped out the door and headed toward the elevator. I didn't hear Vance's door click shut behind me. I glanced back and sure enough, he was standing in the doorway watching me. I gave him a small wave and stepped into the elevator. Safe, for now.

• • •

I was hit with the stench of Val's perfume as soon as I walked into our room. Tessa had opened the window, but it didn't seem to be helping.

"Why would Val put on so much perfume?" Tessa asked.

"No idea. Actually, I take that back. I do know. She told me perfume was ghost repellent."

"That can't be true," Tessa said.

"Val has some crazy ideas. Maybe she's right. I haven't seen a single ghost. But listen to this—you're not going to believe what I saw in Vance's room."

"That's probably true. I haven't believed most of what has happened this weekend was possible."

I fell onto my bed. I had to be careful, so that I didn't crush Gumdrop when I landed. He'd decided to sleep on my pillow, as usual, since he always tries to find the comfiest place to sleep.

"It was full of bondage gear," I said, not wanting to elaborate.

Tessa stared at me in silence.

"I know, I'm speechless too," I said.

"He doesn't seem like the type. And neither does his wife," said Tessa.

"You think they could be bizarre enough to kill someone?"

"You know, when we decided to come to the bead bazaar, I didn't think it would be the *bead bizarre*."

"Are we adding Vance and Lin to the suspect list?" Tessa asked.

Gumdrop decided my lap looked more comfortable than the pillow and curled up on my thighs. My cat thought he was psychic, or more accurately, I thought he was. He once told me I needed to leave Miami and move to Seattle, and for that I would be forever grateful. Other than giving me that advice, he hadn't been able to help me solve crimes, or any other problems, for that matter. I figured I might as well try and ask him for help.

"Okay, Gummie. There must be a reason why you're here," I said, holding him up by his armpits (front-leg-pits?) so I could look into his giant green eyes. He didn't look happy, which was usual. "Do you know who killed Saundra?"

Gumdrop just stared at me. Nothing. Then he wriggled out of my grip.

"So much for Gumdrop and his telepathic communication," Tessa said as Gumdrop jumped onto her lap. He clearly wanted to be far enough away from me that I couldn't reach him and put him into that undignified position again.

"We're just going to have to rely on our own brains to find the killer, since Gummie is uncooperative," I said. "Detective Houston said that if I didn't cooperate with her—not just cooperate but actually help her—she was going to cuff me and parade me around the bead sale so all my friends could see me being dragged off to jail."

Val burst in the door.

"Helloooo, my darlings," Val said, as she sank down on the foldout bed we'd ordered. "Has there been any paranormal activity in here since you arrived?"

"No, Val, it's all ghost-free here," Tessa said.

"Are you sure?" Val asked, pulling a chrome-colored bottle of perfume from her purse.

"No. It's fine in here, still plenty smelly—" Tessa said.

"What Tessa means is fragrant. It's plenty fragrant in here to keep anyone—"

"—any *ghosts* from bothering us," Tessa finished for me.

"Okay, I'll just leave the bottle here, in case you need it," Val said.

"Did you learn anything at the bead bazaar?" I asked Val.

"I did," Val said, taking off her high heels and rubbing her feet. "First I went to Dark Star beads."

"That would be Lara and Sara."

"Those girls could use a makeover. All of that black. Yuck." Val was notorious for wanting to fix everyone's fashion statements, including mine. While she succeeded in helping me embrace my curviness, I was never going to look as glamorous as Val.

I rolled my eyes. "But did you learn anything?"

"They don't like anyone, and they were not being discreet about it. They sat at their table and criticized every single person in the room."

"None of that puts them in the running as the killers. Hating everyone is not a good reason to murder a particular person," Tessa said.

"But, there was one thing," Val said. "They were arguing about something, but I couldn't hear enough to understand what it was."

That was mysterious. Those two were alike in every way. At least in how they looked and how they acted. But what about what they *thought*? They could have different opinions about all sorts of things.

"I also stopped by Vandal's booth. There was some geeky guy there with his Asian wife," Val said.

"That would be Vandal," I said.

"He doesn't look like a Vandal."

"Looks can be deceiving," I said. "His real name is Vance."

"I didn't get much of anything from them. He seemed upset that he had come to the show, like he hadn't made enough money to make it worth his while. And something about how at least they'd get to take some advertising photos in some of the sketchier neighborhoods in Portland. Whatever that meant."

"That's the thing. You should see all the props they have in their room. They dress up his wife in bondage gear and…"

"How naughty! I would never have thought that of those two."

"According to Vance, all those gizmos are just for the photos, not for anything kinky," I said.

"And then I stopped by Minnie's booth." Val continued her recap of her sleuthing mission. "Everything seemed fine there. Minnie has a helper in her booth who is super-cute in that hipster sort of way."

"Miles? Do you really think so? I thought he looked kind of nerdy," I said.

"He's got a certain style. It works for him," Val said, shrugging.

"I always thought it seemed like he was trying a little too hard to look cool," Tessa added.

"Minnie and Miles were whispering and smiling a lot, but I didn't get any sense that either of them was going out and killing people," Val said.

"And poor Minnie, when I found her in the bathroom yesterday morning, she was really upset. She told me Saundra was a treasure," I said.

"Usually people, whether they're guilty or innocent, try and make it look like they're not violent killers," Tessa pointed out. "Of course she'd be upset, or at least try and act upset."

"What about Miles? Saundra was awful to him." I interrupted myself before Tessa started berating me again for speaking ill of the dead.

"Saundra didn't treat Miles well. But that doesn't mean he'd kill her. After all, without Saundra, he didn't have a job," Tessa said.

"What about Indigo?" I asked. "Her table was near Saundra's. Did you talk with her?"

"She was sitting by herself and making a bracelet. It was so pretty, I bought it. See?" said Val, jingling it in my face. "Indigo, she's too nice to kill anyone. She sold me the bracelet for half price."

I needed to remember that I can influence Val by simply giving her a pretty piece of jewelry.

"I spent a long time with Wendy," Val said. "That woman is obsessed with polka-dots."

"Apparently she's been that way for years," I said.

"I had a super-nice talk with her. She seems really upset about Saundra. Sounds like they've been friends for most of their lives."

"Like me and Tessa," I said.

"Yes, and like you and I will be someday, after we live next door to each other for the rest of our lives," Val said.

"I'm not planning on moving, are you?" I asked.

"No way, Jax, you're stuck with me."

Val rattled off all the rest of the information she'd gathered. The end result included things I already knew: The Twins hated everyone. Minnie and Miles were experiencing hipster love. Vance and Lin were a strange couple. And Indigo didn't have any idea about how to make a profit.

None of that got me any closer to finding a suspect or helping Ryan solve this case. I wanted to help Tiffany, too, but only because she was forcing me to be on her team. And ultimately, we were all on the same team, trying to find a killer before he, or she, struck again.

"Did you see Sal?" I asked. "He's the show promoter. He wouldn't have been at a booth, just walking around like he owns the place."

"Is he the one with a scrawny neck? Looks like an alien from the Star Wars Cantina?"

"That's not Sal. That's Ernie, the electrician."

Too bad Val hadn't been able to talk with Sal. Val and Sal, a match made in heaven. Sal would love Val with her voluptuous curves. In my mind, Sal was the number one suspect, since Saundra cost him a lot of money when she was a no-show at her class in LA. Apparently, in other people's minds, I was the number one suspect. I was looking forward to proving them wrong.

"Thanks, Val. You tried, but I don't think this got us anywhere."

"You know, when I was at your booth, I saw the book you were selling. It's got a bead that looks like a galaxy on the cover," Val said.

"That's Saundra's bead, the lady who wrote the *Celestial Bead Designs* book— the one who died."

"That's funny," Val said, removing a pouch from her gold lamé purse. She pulled open the bag, and a bead tumbled into her hand. "It's just like this bead."

Tessa gasped. "Where did you get that bead?"

"All the beads that were in Saundra's booth were confiscated by the police," I said.

"I didn't buy it here. It came from the Saturday Market."

I looked closely at the bead. It was nearly perfect, with just a small smudge on one side. It was exactly like the Cosmos beads that Saundra made.

"Who'd you buy it from?" I asked.

"A girl, she looked like maybe she was in her early thirties, wearing a striped shirt. I remember that because I was thinking how she'd never learned that she shouldn't wear stripes and patterns. She had her hair pulled back in a big floral scarf. You know I always judge people by their hair—if she'd had a cute style, it could have made up for her bad fashion choices—"

"Val, slow down. Did you get a business card? Anything?"

"Sorry, I didn't get her name. She wanted cash, and so I gave her forty dollars for it," Val said. "I thought Rudy would like it—since he loves all the same outer space movies that I do."

Someone was making Cosmos beads, and I was pretty sure it wasn't Saundra.

NINETEEN

"TESSA AND I ARE GOING to dinner and karaoke with her friend Adriana. Do you want to join us?" I asked Val.

"We are?" Tessa asked.

"Adriana wouldn't take no for an answer," I said.

"Wish I could do it, girls, but I've got a date," said Val.

"A date? You've been here only a few hours and you have a date?"

"Oh yes, that sexy guy with the cute Australian accent who sells those necklaces in the last row of the bazaar."

"No, Val. No. You can't go out with Luke," I said, sitting next to her on the fold-out bed and shaking my head. "He's a notorious ladies' man."

"He's got this thing that he does. When I was trying on necklaces, he lifted the hair off my neck and draped the necklace around me. His hands caressed my neck as he adjusted the necklace." Val sighed, closing her eyes. "So sexy. Then he said—"

"Val, we know what he does. He says you look magnificent, and the necklace is perfect for your perfect face," I said.

"Yes, that *was* what he said," Val said, astounded.

"He says that to every woman when he puts a necklace on her," I said.

"He sells a lot of necklaces," Tessa added with a knowing nod.

"It's not like I'm going to marry him," Val said. "And besides, I didn't buy a necklace from him."

"I'm glad he didn't sell you anything," Tessa said.

"I didn't have to, he gave me this," she said, holding up a shiny strand of beads made with dichroic glass—a type of glass that has been coated to be extra-sparkly. Dichroic beads shimmer in an iridescent rainbow of colors. No wonder Val liked the necklace. It was the glitziest piece of jewelry at the sale.

"Wow, that *is* a nice piece. Wonder what it will cost you later tonight?" I asked, in a tone that sounded like I knew she'd end up sleeping with him before the night was over.

"Can we talk a little more about dinner and a little less about Val's love life? I'm starving," Tessa said.

I couldn't stop thinking about the bead Val had purchased at the Saturday Market. Where did it come from? Who sold it to Val?

"Tessa, I'll meet you at the restaurant. It's Club Arigato. I think it's on Stark," I said.

"Where are you headed?" Tessa asked.

"To the Saturday Market."

• • •

I ran as fast as I could to the market, arriving at the end of the street where the vendors' tents were set up. I was out of breath and stopped for a minute, leaning up against a fire plug, panting. The vendors were folding up their tents and packing their handcrafted candles, T-shirts, soaps, and scarves into boxes. I hoped to find out something from my trip down here—find the mysterious woman who was selling Saundra's beads, or who was making beads that looked just like Saundra's. But it looked like I might be too late. Everyone was closing up for the night.

I walked down one aisle, looking for anyone selling beads and jewelry. When I got to the end of that row, I turned and walked all the way back up the next row of booths, now mostly disassembled.

By the time I made it back to the fire plug where I had started, it was nearly dark. I was out of luck, and it was time to get over to the restaurant to meet Tessa, Adriana, and all the rest of the people who were crazy enough to sing in public.

As I turned to leave, I ran into a young woman. She looked up at me, and I saw it: A Cosmos bead hanging on a cord around her neck.

"Where did you get that bead?" I asked.

She didn't answer, just turned and bolted, flipping up the hood on her long sweater as she merged into the crowd of sellers who were packing up the last of their items. She slipped between two pop-up sales tents and out of sight. I tried to follow her out through the tents and into the streets. It was fully dark now, and I walked past street after street, looking down each to see if I could catch sight of the woman.

Who was she? I'd never seen her before at bead bazaars or classes. Had she made those beads, ripping off designs that Saundra created? Had she stolen those beads from the bead diva? Or was there some other explanation?

As Val had said, the woman was wearing a floral scarf. But when I saw her, the scarf had slid back on her head, revealing one important way of identifying her in the future: Her hair was green.

Another thing I was sure of was that I had no idea where I was. I'd gone running off in search of the mystery bead seller and was now so far away from the market that I didn't recognize any of the street names. I pulled my cell phone out of my handbag. The batteries were dead. I would get no help from the GPS tonight.

I zigzagged my way back to the promenade by the Willamette River and walked down the silent, broad sidewalk. Since I didn't think I'd ever be able to find the karaoke bar, I headed toward the hotel—at least I hoped I was headed in the right direction. As I continued, I heard footsteps behind me, and they were getting closer. And closer.

I picked up my pace, and the steps behind me followed, faster. I cut across the street—I heard my stalker's steps quicken and follow me. My best choice was to get out of there as fast as I could. I picked up my pace, jogging.

TWENTY

"JAX!"

"What are you doing here?" I asked Ryan, as I stopped running, out of breath.

"I was just heading to work," he said.

"Were you stalking me?"

"Stalking, that's a pretty strong word," Ryan said.

"You didn't just run into me by accident, did you?"

"No, I was just trying to keep you safe. I was tailing you. It's a police thing. Apparently I'm not doing it well, because if I were, you wouldn't have known I was behind you."

I wasn't the only one who was stealth-impaired.

"Ah, that's sweet," I said, looking up into his warm mocha-brown eyes.

"I like you, and I wouldn't want you to get hurt out here on the streets of Portland," Ryan said, stepping close to me. I stepped backward until I was pressed against the brick wall behind me.

"Portland doesn't seem that scary to me," I said, recalling some of the scary places I'd visited late at night. Most recently, Tessa and I found ourselves driving up and down The Ave in Seattle, surrounded by all sorts of seedy types. "Of course, I'm feeling lots safer now."

"Are you cold?" he asked.

I nodded. Now that I'd stopped running, I realized how cold I was. Ryan took off his leather jacket and wrapped it around my shoulders. His hands were warm, and I was feeling, I must admit, sweaty and tingly all over, but that may have been from jogging.

"Ah, this feels really good," I said, pulling the jacket around me.

"I could show you some other things that might really warm you up," Ryan said with a sly smile, tugging on the collar of the coat and moving even closer, just inches away.

"Ryan."

"Ryan," I said, trying again.

"Sorry, I was getting carried away with some less than respectable thoughts." He stepped back, abashed. "I couldn't help myself, you're just so…"

"So…?"

"Adorable."

Adorable?

I'd never been called adorable. The most I'd ever been called was cute, so *adorable* was a step in the right direction.

"Let's just take a moment here," I said, pressing my hands to his chest, ready to push him back. He was wearing a flannel shirt, and it was soft and warm. While I loved a man in a uniform, it turns out what I really, really love is a man in a flannel shirt. Surprised to realize this so late in life, I was glad I'd moved to the Pacific Northwest. I certainly would never have found anyone wearing flannel in Florida—except for crazy old guys who lived in the Everglades, and I was pretty sure I didn't want to date any of them.

"I was heading back to the hotel, but now that you're here, maybe you can help me get to Club Arigato," I said, realizing that if I spent much more time in such close proximity to Ryan, I'd find myself running my hands up and down his cozy shirt, and more.

"Of course. But are you sure you don't want to find someplace quiet? I've got a little time before I need to be on duty."

"We can pick this up again sometime soon," I said, sliding around him. "Right now, I need to find my friends." And catch my breath.

"I hope we can," he said. "Now, Club Arigato, it's down here a couple blocks."

• • •

Without Ryan, it would have been nearly impossible to find Club Arigato. A tiny sign hung above the door: *Arigato*.

Inside, it wasn't hard to locate my friends. They were the only ones there.

"You're going to stay?" I asked Ryan.

"I'm not working until midnight. I have time to hang out before I start my shift. No alcohol for me, though."

"Sounds good." I could do enough drinking for the both of us.

We found seats next to Tessa, who was sipping sake from a tiny white cup. Ryan pulled a chair up close to me.

"Did you eat?" I asked Tessa.

"Some tempura and California rolls."

When the waitress came, I ordered another round of sake for Tessa and me to share, plus an order of sashimi, and a green tea for Ryan.

"Tessa, have you ever met a beadmaker with green hair?"

"No. Have you?"

"Yes, as a matter of fact, a little while ago. When I was at the Saturday Market, I saw a woman who was wearing a bead just like one of Saundra's. I've never seen her before, and when I tried talking to her, she ran away," I said. "She's either a beadmaker who is copying Saundra's designs and making her own beads, or she's stolen some of Saundra's beads and is selling them."

"That's strange, but green hair doesn't help. You know, she could have green hair this week, and next week she could have purple hair. Do you have anything else to go on?"

"Nothing. I don't even know her name. She didn't seem too happy when I asked her about the bead she was wearing. That's when she ran for it."

The music started up, and the lights dimmed. The disco ball sparkled to life. At the front of the room, a man in a cheap tuxedo grabbed a microphone.

"Laaadies and gentlemennnn, welcome to Club Arigato's world-famous karaoke party," the man shouted in a smooth, overly-modulated voice, as he tilted the mic forward with both hands.

Tessa and I rolled our eyes.

"I'm DJ Dan, your host for this night of special singers. And I want you and you and you," he was now pointing out each of us individually, "to be ready to come up here and give us a performance that will make you proud." Tessa and I looked down at our drinks. It was a technique we'd used in high school math class. We'd focus on our desktops so we didn't make eye contact with the teacher, with the hope she'd not choose us to answer questions. I hoped this situation would be the same—if we didn't make eye contact with DJ Dan, he wouldn't call us up to perform.

"Fiiiirst up is Adrianaaaaa. Let's give it up for this super special lady!"

Adriana started things off with a karaoke classic: "Wind Beneath My Wings." I never liked that song, but I really hated it when Adriana sang it. It turns out that even though she liked singing in public, it didn't mean she was good at it. She warbled like Gumdrop when it was past his dinnertime.

Vance was up next with "Piano Man" by Billy Joel. I wasn't expecting much, but the guy really knew how to sing. He belted that song out. How was that possible? Vance was just full of surprises. Nobody really knew much about him. Who knew what else he was capable of?

"Do you think Vance could have killed Saundra?" I asked Tessa while we watched him perform. I grabbed a handful of wasabi peanuts and popped a few in my mouth.

"What makes Vance suspicious?" Ryan asked.

"His room is full of torture gear," I said. Ryan's eyes were wide with surprise. "He was only at the bar for a little while that first night. He had plenty of time to find Saundra in the showroom and knock her off."

"All of us had the opportunity to kill Saundra—each of us had periods of time that night that were unaccounted for. Except me. I was with Adriana. Anyone else could have killed her," Tessa said.

"Anyone?" asked Ryan.

"It's hypothetical. It's nearly impossible to rule out anyone based on where they were when Saundra was murdered."

"Maybe Vance knew Saundra from a past bead sale," I said, ignoring Tessa's hypothesis, my focus still on Vance. "Maybe he only decided to come to the show to confront her."

"He'd never been to any other bead sales, remember? Maybe he's just a man who is a little shy and decided to finally face his fear of being in public and signed up to sell beads at a bazaar." Tessa was always so level-headed; she reined in my wild imagination.

The Twins sang next: "Girlfriend in a Coma" by The Smiths. The song started with a light guitar riff before swinging into lyrics about murder and strangulation, which was disturbing, to say the least, after my awful experience with a dead body the day before. The Twins sang in an oddly harmonic and creepy style, perfect for the song. Tessa was looking down into her empty sake cup, likely trying to decide whether to fill it up again. I couldn't tell if she was paying attention to the song's dark message.

"Tessa," I whispered, hoping she was listening to the lyrics. "They're singing about killing someone." I received no response from her.

To get her attention, I elbowed Tessa a little harder than I meant to—so hard she almost fell out of her seat.

"Ow!" Everyone looked over at Tessa. "Ohhh! Woo! Woo!" she corrected, as she starting clapping, trying to make her pain look like an exclamation of approval for the song.

"I didn't deserve that," Tessa said, pouring the last of the sake into her cup.

"Sorry—do you think it was The Twins? Could they have murdered Saundra?"

"I think you have murder on the brain. Just try to enjoy the show and watch our friends making fools of themselves, okay?"

I turned to Ryan. "Are you going to sing?" I asked.

"No, I'm not much of a singer. But I'm enjoying watching everyone perform."

"Me, too."

"And I'm enjoying being here with you," he said, scooting his chair a little closer to mine.

"Me, too," I said as I leaned toward him. He put his arm around me.

Next up was Lin, who quietly took the stage. She whispered her music selection to the DJ, and the music started. Lin shouted the lyrics to "Hit Me With Your Best Shot" by Pat Benatar while wildly jumping up and down to the beat. We were shocked by her rendition.

Vance was sitting in front of me. I tapped him on the shoulder and gestured wildly, trying to say, "I'm surprised," "I'm shocked," and "I'm impressed" all at once.

He smiled enigmatically and said only, "Oh yes, Lin's unpredictable."

I didn't think she would be so outrageous on stage, or in the bedroom, but then again, looks can be deceiving. I'd learned that when I discovered all the scary costumes and bondage gear in the hotel room she shared with Vance.

When Lin's song ended, she politely curtsied and left the stage, taking her seat next to Vance.

"Jax, I've got to hit the road," Ryan said.

"You're really not going to sing?"

"No time. Maybe I can sing for you some other time, in private."

"I'll stop by the ballroom a little later."

"Just as long as you don't want in," he added, joking.

"Ryan, do you mind if I come with you?" Tessa asked. "It's been a long day, and I'm tired." She'd also had a few cups of sake and was getting sleepy from the alcohol, I expected.

"Sure," said Ryan. "Any friend of Jax's is a friend of mine." I watched as Tessa, my oldest friend, headed out the door with my newest friend. I hoped I'd be getting much friendlier with Ryan soon.

"How about you, Jax? Are you going to sing for us?" Adriana asked.

"Oh, no. I'm not allowed to sing in public." It was true. Val had banned me from singing, except in the shower or to sing "Happy

Birthday," ever since I'd tried karaoke at her salon's holiday party. Maybe it was the three glasses of heavily-spiked eggnog that made me sound so terrible. Probably not.

Miles came in a little while later. His over-sized messenger bag was slung over his shoulder, the head of a ukulele case sticking out of the top corner of the bag.

He pulled his ukulele case from his bag, flipped up the square metal clasp to open the lid, and pulled out the tiny guitar. He told DJ Dan he didn't need any accompaniment. And with that, he sat down on the edge of the small stage, with the disco ball spraying silver spots of lights in circles above our heads, and played the most incredible version of "Hotel California" on his tiny instrument. When he was done, we all jumped up and applauded.

"Miles—that was outstanding. I had no idea you were so talented. What an impressive performance. I love that song," I said, still clapping.

"It was supposed to be ironic," Miles said.

"I think it was way more than ironic...it was iconic," I said.

"Encore!" we all shouted.

"Stairway to Heaven" never sounded better than when Miles played it on the uke.

TWENTY-ONE

"THE RED ROSE HOTEL," I told the taxi driver. I didn't want to spend any more time wandering the streets of Portland late at night. With my dead phone and no GPS, I doubted I could have found my way back to the hotel, or anywhere else for that matter.

I took the elevator—still oddly cold inside—up to our floor, making sure I got off at floor six and not floor five. Tessa was walking toward me, her face streaked with tears. I ran to her and hugged her tight.

"Tessa! Sweetie! What happened?" I asked. "Is something going on with the girls? Are they okay? Joey? Craig? Everyone's okay?"

"I…they…someone…a mess…how," Tessa said without making a bit of sense.

"I'm sorry, Tessa, I just don't understand. Try again, one word at a time." She grabbed my hand and turned, pulling me down the hall.

"Our…room…" Tessa pushed hard on the door. Inside, our room looked like a tornado had hit it.

"What happened?" I felt a small guilty twinge, wondering if the scary maid I'd encountered outside Saundra's room had discovered which room was mine and decided to seek revenge. Gumdrop was in this room somewhere, probably scared to death. At least I hoped he was still in there.

"I don't know what happened. I came back to the room after karaoke and opened the door, and it was like this," said Tessa. "I didn't want to go in and mess it up in case there were fingerprints or something."

"So you decided to stand around in the hall, until *what* happened?"

"I called the front desk and told them our room was a mess. They offered to send up housekeeping, but I didn't think that was appropriate," Tessa said. "I called you ten times—you never answered. I sat here, waiting for you to get one of my messages, and trying to figure out how to find Ryan or the detective. Then I thought I should just go back downstairs…"

"I'm sorry, my phone was dead. I forgot to charge it."

Tessa wiped the tears off her nose with her sleeve. She would have scolded one of her children if they had done the same.

The elevator doors opened. Ryan sprinted down the hall toward us.

"I heard someone at the front desk say there was a problem in your room. What happened?"

Tessa waved a hand toward the doorway of our wrecked room.

Ryan peered into the room and exhaled a long low whistle. "That's a mess. I wonder what the person who did this was looking for."

"A clue? Money? I don't have either," I said.

"This has been a terrible night. I found one of the guards, Carl Shulman, during my security check. He was in the stairwell, his head cracked open, blood everywhere," Ryan said, shaking his head. "Based on the way we found him, he may have been pushed, but the medical examiner will make that determination in the next few days."

I gasped. "You mean he's dead? What was he doing in the stairwell?"

"Carl wasn't very reliable, and he sometimes abandoned his post. It's possible he was coming back from a guest's room. I don't know what he was doing or why he's dead, but I intend to find out. He was a good guy, and his family deserves to know what happened."

"Do you have anything that could point to who might have killed him?"

"I found a bead-shaped plastic keychain with the words *Bead Fun* printed on it next to him on the stairs," Ryan said.

"Can I see it?" I asked, wondering if it was the one I'd seen in Sal's RV.

"I've already given it to Tiff—uh, I mean Detective Houston," Ryan said.

TWENTY-TWO

"IT MUST BE SAL'S KEYCHAIN," I said.

"It's a keychain that Sal made. There could be any number of people who have one. It's just a cheap promotional item," Tessa said.

"It might be a clue—maybe Sal pushed the guy down the stairs," I said.

"Or maybe not, maybe it's nothing, just a random piece of junk on the stairs," Tessa said. She glanced over at our thrashed room. "I don't care about the stupid keychain. I care about getting back in our room and cleaning up this mess."

"You two can't stay here," Ryan told us. "I think this is a crime scene now, given the other incidents that we've had this weekend."

"What are we supposed to do? Where are we supposed to sleep?" asked Tessa, her body tense with anger. Her phone started dinging as text messages popped up on her phone again and again, aggravating her even more.

Ryan unclipped the radio from his belt and called down to the front desk.

"Marie? It's Ryan in Security. We've got a situation up here in room 611. I'm sending you a couple guests who need a new room," Ryan said, then listened to the response. "Okay, thanks, they're on their way."

"Go to the front desk, and Marie will take care of you," Ryan said.

"And what about our belongings?" Tessa asked, sounding calmer now that she knew she'd have a place to sleep tonight.

"Unfortunately, under these circumstances I need to secure the room until the police can gather evidence and look for signs of theft and damage. That means you'll get your things back tomorrow. I will personally make sure that happens."

"I really don't want to have to wear the same clothes two days in a row," I said. If I was going to be the next murder victim, I wanted to heed my mother's advice and have on clean underwear when I showed up in the morgue. Or was that the hospital?

Ryan approached the door to examine the lock and the knob.

"What are we going to do about you-know-who?" I asked Tessa.

"Val? You can text her and let her know where we are."

"No, Tessa," I hissed, grabbing her hand and pulling her a few steps away from Ryan. "I mean the *other guest who is staying in our room.*"

"Gumdrop," she said a little too loudly. My cat was in the room; at least I hoped he was still in there. We needed to get him out. There was no way I was going to leave him behind for the night.

"We're not even supposed to have a cat in our room," Tessa whispered in my ear.

"Ryan, I need to get something out of the room," I said. "It's really important."

"And what is it that can't stay in this room overnight? Valuables?"

"My roommate—not Tessa here—but my other roommate, who frequently breaks all the rules, sort of smuggled a cat into our room."

"A cat?"

"Not just any cat. My cat."

"He's the best cat," said Tessa, trying to be helpful, but I was sure Ryan didn't care what kind of a cat Gummie was.

"You do realize this hotel has a strict no-pet policy?" Ryan asked, with a small laugh that told me he wasn't serious about evicting us for breaking the rules.

"We need to get this room locked up immediately so the investigators can examine it tomorrow," said Ryan, taking a more serious tone.

"I'll go in and get Gummie," I offered. "Val's giant tote is in there too, so I'll just put him in that, and we'll get out of here."

"Sorry, Jax. I think I better get him. You're already a suspect in a murder investigation. I don't think you should spend any more time than is necessary messing around with a crime scene."

Ryan entered the room while Tessa and I watched from the doorway. I was nervous. Gummie wasn't all that friendly with men, having recently attacked a reporter on my sofa during an interview. Although, what Gumdrop really did was attack the drink the reporter was holding, which was laced with catnip.

"Here kitty-kitty-kitty," Ryan said quietly. "Come on out." That Gumdrop did not immediately run out of his hiding place seemed to surprise Ryan. It didn't surprise me at all. Gummie was not one to take orders, and he was more of a saunterer than a runner.

"His name is Gumdrop?" Ryan asked.

"Yes, but also try Gummie." If Gumdrop didn't want to be found, nothing you called him would help.

"Gummie? Gummie? Where are you?" whispered Ryan as he crept around the room, gingerly avoiding stepping on any possible evidence, even stepping around the vacuum cleaner tracks on the carpet. He got down on his hands and knees and looked under the bed.

"A-ha! There you are," said Ryan. "Come on out." Ryan reached under the bed and tried to grab the cat.

A long hiss came from under the bed. Ryan quickly withdrew his hand and retreated.

"I don't think your cat likes me." This was not surprising, given Gummie's recent bad attitude about many things, including being forced to do something he didn't want to do.

"It looks like Gumdrop scratched you," Tessa said. Drops of blood trailed across Ryan's wrist.

In a typical mom move, Tessa whipped out a tissue and a Band-Aid, ready to administer first aid.

"No, I'm fine, really. I don't need anything. It's just a little nick."

Tessa grabbed his hand and applied the Band-Aid. You did not say no to Tessa.

"Look, I'm going to walk away," Ryan said, pressing his Band-Aid down and nodding a thanks to Tessa. "I'm just heading downstairs. I don't want to see you going in the room. Just make sure you close the door when you leave. And take the cat, nothing else."

Standing in the doorway of the room, I pulled Gummie's carrier-cum-tote bag toward me. Val had tossed a couple of cans of cat food into the bag. I pulled a can out and popped off the lid. Immediately, at that distinctive *snick* sound of the can's seal releasing, Gumdrop was at my feet. Gummie may not come when he is called, but he certainly never misses a meal. I grabbed the cat and stuffed him in the carrier along with the can of food.

"Ugh, Gumdrop. I need to put you on a diet," I said, lugging him down the hall as Tessa closed the door and double-checked the lock.

"Yelllloooo" was Gumdrop's only response.

We found Ryan by the front desk. "Here you are, Marie, these are the guests who need a new room for a few nights."

"Okay ladies, what we've got here is a situation. The hotel is completely sold out. Like there are *no* rooms." Marie was typing and talking at the same time, and it was a challenge for her.

"Yes, I see. Usually that is what 'completely sold out' means—that there are no rooms," I said—I admit it—sarcastically. I was tired and cranky at this point and ready for bed. Any bed. Well, maybe not *any* bed.

"But...I've got this one room—"

"We'll take it." We held our hands out for the key card. I hoped we weren't about to move into a broom closet.

"I've got to get back on duty. I'm glad you both are safe," Ryan said. Then turning to me, he said, "See you tomorrow?"

"Oh, yes. See you then," I said, half-wishing I was heading upstairs with him instead of Tessa.

"Enjoy your stay," said Marie, as she slid the tiny envelope containing the key card across the counter toward us with a smile. "Tenth floor."

The key card was marked with a big number ten, but Marie hadn't told us a room number.

"How are we going to know which room is ours?" I asked Tessa as the elevator, as chilly as ever, whisked us past floor after floor.

The elevator's doors clunked open, revealing one door at the end of a short hallway. We slid the key card in and out of the reader, and pushed the door open.

Tessa and I stood in stunned silence, looking into the room. How could we have possibly ended up here?

"Definitely not a broom closet," Tessa said, breaking the silence.

I was astounded by the gorgeous room in front of us. It was exquisite, filled with elegant mahogany furniture, and a vibrant Oriental rug in greens and blues. A wet-bar stood along one wall, and there was a gorgeous view of the city expanding before us behind floor-to-ceiling windows.

"I sure hope we're not paying for this," I said, looking at the rate card posted on the inside of the door. "Because if we have to pay, you'll need to sell off your first-born child."

"Selling her off sounds like a pretty good idea. And my second-born, too," Tessa said, collapsing on the sofa.

"I fully agree. I actually think if you have the opportunity to sell off both of your daughters to settle our hotel bill, we could give them a pretty good deal. Maybe two for the price of one?" I said as I looked around the luxurious suite. I stepped into the bathroom. It was tiled with luscious crema marfil tile and finished with brushed nickel hardware. Plush sage-green towels, many more than we could use, were stacked in an alcove near an oversized claw-footed tub.

"Oh, my, Tessa, you're going to have to see this," I said, leaning out of the bathroom door. "It's the most beautiful bathroom I've ever seen." There was another door that led to a bedroom with two elegant queen-sized beds. Each was covered in so many layers of quilts and pillows I'd almost need a ladder to crawl on top of it.

"Tessa? This sure beats our old room with its shabby bedspreads and stained carpet," I said, laughing with astonishment. I turned around to see if I had succeeded in cheering up Tessa. I found her fast asleep, head tipped back on the sofa cushions. I removed her shoes and flopped her down on the couch. I wasn't going to try and get her into a bed. I found a soft wool blanket in the closet and covered her up. "Goodnight, Tessa. Tomorrow will be a better day."

TWENTY-THREE

I BORROWED TESSA'S PHONE and called Val to tell her where our new room was. She was at our door a few minutes later.

"Are you going to tell me what you've been up to?" I said as I let Val in.

"Luke was super nice." Of course he was. "And he bought me a drink," Val said, sashaying into the room. "And then we—"

"Val, I don't want to hear about it."

"Niiiiice. Who'd you have to sleep with to get this room?" Val asked with a little wink. "That super hot security guy?"

"I'm not going to talk about that. And it's not like you've got any moral superiority. You've been dating Rudy, and now you're out with Luke, having drinks and doing who knows what—"

"I'm not dating Rudy. It's platonic. You know what that means, right? It's the same thing I tried to tell Bruno."

I stood there, looking at her blankly. I'd never heard her say she was having a relationship with a man that didn't involve sleeping with him.

"You know, Jax? Platonic, as in *just a friend*, like you and me."

"Yes, Val, I know what platonic means. It's just surprising. I didn't think you had friends who are guys. And Luke, what's the story with him?"

"Luke, he's a passionate man. He needs someone like me to be passionate with him."

"Val, I don't want to hear about it."

"Oh no! Where's Gumdrop?" Val asked, looking around. "You didn't leave him behind in the old room, did you?"

"Of course not. He's already curled up on my bed."

"Where do I get to sleep? Looks like Tessa's already got the sofa," Val said, noticing Tessa passed out on the couch.

"There's a bedroom with two queen beds. Take the one without the cat."

With her leopard print overnight bag on her shoulder, Val headed into the room.

"Time for bed," said Val, peering out the door at me. "You need some beauty sleep."

"I look that bad, huh?"

"Oh, nothing a few hours of rest can't cure."

In her pink satin nightie, Val stood at the bathroom mirror taking off her makeup. My tinted lip balm and mascara had worn off hours ago. She finished her beauty regimen, got in bed, and pulled on her zebra-print eye mask.

"Night-night, honey."

"Good night, Val." It was quiet and dark in the room, but I couldn't sleep. My beauty sleep, or any kind of sleep, was going to have to wait.

I slid out of bed and into my jeans.

TWENTY-FOUR

I DIDN'T KNOW what to expect in Le Bar so late at night. I hoped some of my friends from the bazaar would be there. It would be nice to have a drink and chat with someone—and not the kind of chat that Detective Houston liked to have.

There was one person in the bar, and while he wasn't my favorite person in the world, he might just have some answers for me. Sal.

"Uh, hi, Sal," I said, coming up behind him. He turned, surprised, and then his face turned from surprise to lecherous delight.

"Coming to find me, eh? You wanna go back to my trailer?" he asked.

"Look, Sal, it's not what you think. I was trying to see if any of my friends might be down here. And instead, it's just...you."

"Oh baby, you're just being shy now," Sal said, beckoning me to sit next to him at the low slung table next to the bar's balcony railing.

"Just hold on, Sal." I sat down across the table from him, well out of arm's reach. I might as well make use of this time, since I had several questions for Sal.

"Here, lemme buy you a drink. Whaddya want?" Sal asked, getting up and heading to the bar.

"Nothing, I'm fine."

"Suit yourself," Sal said. He ordered and paid for his drink, then slid back into his seat with a new double bourbon in his hand. Sal looked like a bullfrog, half-lidded eyes staring straight ahead, not moving, but not uncomfortable either. Just sitting, perhaps waiting for a fly to zoom past. I was hoping I wasn't the fly. He'd definitely cooled to me now that he knew I wasn't in the bar looking for a late night hook up.

I looked over the railing and down to the lobby below. Ryan was standing by the ballroom door and talking with another security guard. He glanced up and saw me. And Sal.

"Jax?" Ryan said, staring at us in disbelief.

"Really Ryan, it's not what it looks like," I said in a panic. This was the last thing I needed, for Ryan to see me here with Sal.

"It sure *is* what it looks like," Sal said, scooting his chair around to my side of the table and trying to put his arm around me. "Sorry, pal, she came looking for me. You're missing out."

I looked at Ryan with bulging eyes and mouthed the words, "No, no, no."

"What's going on up there?" Ryan demanded.

"I came here to see if I could have a drink and talk to some friends, but nobody was here except Sal. I have some questions for him, but he thinks I have other things on my mind."

"Oh, yes. We were just heading out to my RV," Sal lied, wriggling an eyebrow.

"Jax? You're going to his RV?" Ryan asked.

"No."

"Fine, you want to ask me something, then do it. Otherwise I'm going back to my trailer to watch the Playboy Channel."

Ryan bounded up the stairs to the bar. He wanted to be a part of this discussion.

"Aren't you supposed—" I gestured toward the ballroom door below.

"I left Paul down there to take care of things. He's our new guy. I think he can handle it for a while. And besides, what else could go wrong?" That was a motto I did not want to explore. What else could go wrong? Another dead body, perhaps?

Ryan pulled up a chair between me and Sal.

"Hey, what's happening here? I was talking with the lady." Sal pushed Ryan away. "Hey, Jax, let's get out of here. I liked it when you came to my RV with that babe. She was a cop, right? I'd sure be happy if she—"

Ryan looked over at me, eyes wide. "You've been to his RV?"

I ignored Ryan's question. "Sal, I'm not going anywhere with you. I need to know a couple things. You want the crime scene tape removed and things back to normal at the bazaar? The best way to do that is to help the police—to help us—with the murder investigation."

"Yeah, all right, all right."

"Can I ask you about Saundra's class—the one that was canceled? When she didn't show up for class, was everyone angry?"

"Yeah, those bead ladies, they can get nasty," Sal said, tossing back his drink. "Look, I was pissed off. The broads were angry, too. And like I told you before, Luke was the worst of them—threatened to sue me. I told him to get out of my face. He lost a lot of money, but I couldn't help him, ya know? You want to check out someone as a murderer, you should look at Luke."

"And you, you lost money too?" I asked.

"Six grand, and believe me, I needed that money. I'd already paid for the hotel and the conference room, so I didn't get that money back. It was a dead loss." Sal stopped, clearly realizing he needed to say something that wouldn't incriminate him. "But, the money I lost, Saundra said she'd make it up to me, that she'd teach a free workshop. Even gave me a contract for the next class—she was droppin' her fee."

I had witnessed that transaction when I first arrived to set up my table. Sal and Saundra had a heated discussion, and then Sal left with an envelope. It must have been the contract for the make-up class. It looked like Sal may not have been Saundra's killer, but what about the other dead body found just hours ago? I decided to ask, although I didn't know how much longer Sal would be willing to talk with us.

"What do you know about Carl Shulman?" I asked.

"Never heard of the guy."

"Carl had your keychain with him when Ryan saw him last." I wanted to see if Sal already knew if Carl was dead. Maybe he'd reveal something that would tell us that he was the guard's killer.

"So? Everybody's got my stupid key chain. Free promotions."

"Carl is dead, Sal," Ryan said.

"Ah, crap—" said Sal.

"Did you know him?" I asked.

"Nah. But it sucks that the guy's dead." Sal reached toward his forehead with one hand. I swear he was going to make the sign of the cross. Instead, he scratched his nose, likely realizing that he wouldn't look like a tough guy if he did something so overtly religious. "Sorry you got another dead guy to deal with. But, you know, I'm hoping you can take care of this quietly. Another dead body ain't good for sales. You gotta know I make a percentage from every vendor. More sales, more money in my pocket."

"I know, because I'm one of your vendors," I said. I would never work with him again and I wished I hadn't made so much money this weekend. Less for me would mean less for Sal.

"Yeah, I know that. The dead guy—he was a vendor?"

"A security guard," Ryan said. "He worked with me."

"Look, Sal, if you know anything, it's important you tell us. You don't want any more cops around here spoiling the buyers' moods," I said.

"I got nothing else for you, I'm outta here." Sal stood, pushing his chair back so forcefully that it nearly toppled over backward.

Ryan and I were left alone in the bar. "That was quite an impressive bit of questioning you did back there. Maybe you should consider a career in law enforcement," Ryan said.

"No, not me. I can barely keep myself and my cat in line. Trying to enforce order on any more than that would be too much of a responsibility."

"I could see why Sal wanted you to come into his RV. I'd let you into my RV anytime."

"You own an RV?" I was hoping his answer would be *no*.

"No." What a relief. "Can I show you something spectacular?" Ryan asked me.

"Sure, what is it?" I was hoping that what I was about to see did not involve him removing any clothing because he was becoming impossible to resist.

"It's more like *where is it?*"

Ryan took my hand and guided me to a service elevator behind the bar's drink preparation area. He pressed the glowing button next to the doors. Once we were inside, Ryan pressed RT.

"RT?"

"It stands for Really Terrific. It's the most terrific floor in the whole building."

When the elevator stopped, the doors slid open abruptly, revealing a tiny roof-top garden. Of course, RT meant roof-top. On all sides, we could see the city of Portland: lights of office buildings, houses, the river and its bridges, and tiny boats with their lights bobbing. The sky was clear, and overhead, we could see a dome of stars and a round golden moon illuminating the garden with a soft glow. We said nothing as we sat on a wooden bench in the center of the garden, potted rose bushes on either side of us.

"It's beautiful here," I said.

"You're beautiful, too."

"Ryan, you really know how to charm a lady," I said, looking out at the city sparkling in front of me.

"You mean, it's working?"

"Yes, you're definitely becoming one of my favorite things about Portland," I said. "After the coffee. And the hipsters. And—"

"Jax, will you just be quiet for minute so I can kiss you?"

I said nothing. And he kissed me. A tingle ran down my spine.

"Wow. That was nice, I mean, wow," I stammered.

"Shhh," Ryan said, kissing me again.

"I could get used to this."

"Me, too," said Ryan. "But…"

"What?"

"I need to get back to Paul. I don't want to leave him alone for too long on his first day—or night—on the job. Let me escort you to your door. It's only down a flight of stairs from where we are," said Ryan, standing and playfully offering me his hand, like a proper suitor.

Time to go back to my beautiful penthouse room and sleep with Gumdrop while I listened to the buzzing of Val's lady-like snores.

TWENTY-FIVE

I WOKE UP ON Sunday morning to the sound of someone knocking on the door of our suite. I shrugged on the hotel's fluffy white robe, hustled to the door, and looked through the peephole. When I saw Ryan's handsome face, I let him in.

"Okay, ladies, here's what I have for you. Jax, I've got a latte," he said. "And I've got donuts." Ryan set a pink box down on the small round table by the floor-to-ceiling windows. He pulled the curtains open. Glorious sunlight spilled into the room.

"Oh, Ryan," I said, giving him a hug. "You're the best."

"That's what all the women say," Ryan said with a grin.

"And for Tessa, I have an espresso. I got you a double because I thought you could use it. With lots of sugar because that's how you like it."

"Oh man, Ryan, if I weren't married, I'd—" said Tessa, straightening up the sofa where she had slept last night.

"Tessa, let's just skip that sentiment, shall we?" I interrupted.

"But how'd you know how I like my coffee?" Tessa asked.

"Ryan's just really perceptive." I wanted to avoid telling Tessa that Ryan sampled her espresso yesterday morning and thought it was so sweet he couldn't drink it. I, for one, could drink any kind of coffee, except, maybe, if it was made with swamp water. Then again, it might depend on the circumstances.

Val traipsed out of the bedroom, pulling a pink satin robe closed over her matching nightie.

"And I'm sorry," Ryan said. "I didn't realize you had another guest staying in the room."

As if on cue, Gummie came strolling out of the bedroom.

"Right, I forgot about your cat. You've got *two* additional guests staying in the room."

"Ryan, this is Val. She had a crisis at home, so she came down, and she brought my cat," I said, trying to reiterate that I had nothing to do with why we had a cat in our room.

"I don't know how you feel about a plain old cup of coffee, but I'll happily give you mine," Ryan said.

"Oh my goodness," Val said, her hand fluttering at her chest. "Aren't you the sweetest, most precious..." Val headed toward him. Tessa grabbed her hand and pulled her onto the sofa next to her, in an effort to keep her from doing anything inappropriate to Ryan. I was thankful for Tessa's interception.

"You're a darling," Val said. "But I'm going to head downstairs in a little while and get something delicious to drink."

"Any chance you brought our clothes?" I asked.

"As a matter of fact, I did," Ryan told us, reaching back into the hallway and grabbing our suitcases.

"You're a superstar," I said, giving him a kiss. We lingered just a little longer than was appropriate. Anyone who brings me donuts and coffee could get anything he wanted from me. Well, almost anything.

Tessa and Val looked at each other, eyes bulging and mouths open in surprise. Val saw the pink bakery box, opened it, and grabbed for a donut.

"Oh my. What is this?" Val squealed, pulling out a long bar-shaped donut with a scary face drawn on it with frosting and stick pretzels poking out of the dough in a couple places.

"It's a voodoo doll from this terrific place called Voodoo Donuts," Ryan said.

Val took a big bite. Red goo seeped out from inside the donut.

"Filled with raspberry jelly, so it looks like blood. That's a nice touch," said Val. "I'll have to think about what I could fill with jelly like this."

The jam looked a little too much like real blood. I knew that wasn't the donut for me.

Tessa looked into the box warily. "I hope there are no more scary donuts in there."

"No, that's the only one, but there's one with bacon," Ryan said. I reached in and grabbed it.

"And this one is covered in Cap'n Crunch," Tessa said, choosing that one and taking a big bite.

"I'll let you ladies get ready for your day. I've got to meet with Detective Houston," said Ryan. "With any luck, she and I will be able to put our heads together and get both of these murders wrapped up shortly."

So, I wasn't the only one on Team Tiffany. So was Ryan. But it wasn't surprising that Ryan's job required that he work with the local police department when crimes occurred at the hotel.

"Here's my number in case you need me," Ryan said. He pulled a page off the note pad on the desk, jotted down his number, and handed it to me. Then he pulled me close, ready to kiss me good-bye. Tessa and Val were trying to eat their donuts and pretending to be paying no attention to us, but doing a bad job of it as they kept stealing glances our way.

"See you later," Ryan said, smoothing out the collar of my robe, then closing the door behind him.

"Ooooh, Jax. I think that boy likes you," said Val. "And such a hottie, too."

I looked at Tessa, waiting for her to chime in.

"I'm not saying a word," said Tessa, shaking her head and popping a stray piece of Cap'n Crunch into her mouth.

"I'm going to get ready and head on down to the bazaar. But first I'm going to eat another donut," I said, peeking in the pink box. "Let's see, which one?"

TWENTY-SIX

"VAL, ARE YOU COMING down to the ballroom with us?" I asked.

"Sure, I'll come for a little while. I thought I might help out Luke in his booth," Val said. "And Luke, it's such a hot name. You know, in *Star Wars*, Luke Skywalker? His original name was Luke—"

"How about helping me out in *my* booth?" I asked.

"—Starkiller. But the film studio changed it. The original name was too dark for such a heroic character."

"Can you focus for a second? I'm trying to help solve a murder here," I told Val. "I need help at my table."

"You're fine. You've got Tessa," Val said. "Doesn't she, Tessa?"

Tessa had her eyes on the phone, reading an endless string of text messages from Izzy and Ashley. When she heard her name, she looked up. "What? What did I miss?"

I finally dragged Val and Tessa out of the room. As we stood in the elevator, we once again felt a chill, stronger this time than we'd ever felt before. Val rummaged around in her giant metallic purse, then pulled out a bottle of perfume and started spraying.

I waved my hands and tried to get the scent to dissipate. "Ugh, Val, that will get rid of more than just ghosts."

"Don't come crying to me if you see a poltergeist." Val dropped the bottle back into her purse.

Tessa and I stood silently, trying not to breathe too deeply. As the elevator doors opened to the lobby, the waiting crowd backed away from the wafts of perfume that followed us and decided to take the next elevator. I didn't blame them. I was going to smell like Val for the rest of the week, and I wasn't sure I liked that.

The lobby was full of customers, armed and ready for another day of treasure hunting at the bazaar. Many had rolling bags they planned to fill, their sneakers on, and a cup of coffee in a travel mug. From the bright eyes and chatter, I could tell they were already well-caffeinated. These were serious beaders, ready to fight for the good stuff if necessary.

The hotel had stationed a grouchy security guard with a Middle Eastern accent at the door to the ballroom. He was checking each vendor's badge carefully.

We moved in a line to the door.

"Where iz your bahdge?" the guard asked Val, with his thick accent.

"Oh, I don't need a badge, do I, honey?"

"You're not a bendor, you got no bendor bahdge."

"What do you mean, I'm 'not a bender'? I'll have you know that I am very bendable."

I pulled Val aside. "Val, you can't come in until the doors open and the public comes in. You're not a *vendor*."

"Well, that makes sense. It made absolutely no sense when he accused me of not being a bender. I'm very bendy, many of my boy-friends have said—"

"Why don't you go get us some coffee?" Usually, I needed a second cup right around now. Actually, I constantly need cups of coffee, and especially after staying up so late last night.

"Good idea. Three coffees coming right up," said Val, flouncing away. She had a lot of flounce for so early in the day.

Tessa and I pulled the sheet off the display, such as it was, dec-orated with things from the hotel room. It had served me well, judging from the terrific sales I'd racked up this weekend.

Looking down at the table, I said, "I hope we don't get charged for all the items we stole—"

"Borrowed," Tessa said. "We certainly would have put them back if we'd stayed in it."

"It wasn't our fault our room was vandalized."

"Vandalized? Vandalized!" Tessa repeated. "Vance? You think Vance could have trashed our room?"

"He was at karaoke with us. How could he?"

"After you left for the Saturday Market, Adriana and I went to Arigato and ate before everyone else got there. He had plenty of time to get into our room."

"I guess we better keep Vance on the list of suspects," I said.

"Just because he trashed our room doesn't mean he would kill a person—or two—"

"Oh, hi, Vance," I said, cutting off Tessa before she revealed we were not only talking about him, we were accusing him of rifling through our belongings and being a killer.

"Here are those lamps you wanted to borrow," Vance said, placing them on the table's edge. "Hope you sell a lot of beads today."

"Thanks. This is really going to help," I said. He really was a nice guy. I had trouble reconciling his sweetness with the scary sex toys in his room.

I moved the lights into position at each end of my table, uncoiled their cords, and plugged them into the toaster-sized power box on the floor. I flicked the switch on one of the lights. Nothing happened. I tried the other one. Nothing.

Ernie the electrician was a few tables down, walking toward me.

"Excuse me. I'm not getting any power to these lights," I told him.

Ernie crawled under the table, grabbed a roll of duct tape from his back pocket and wrapped a long piece of tape around the power box, securing a fist-sized connector to it.

"Sorry, some of these cords, they're getting kind of old. These protective covers keep breaking off." Ernie gave one last push on the power cord. There was a pop, and Vance's lights were now glowing. Everything on my table looked great—shiny and transparent, like glass is supposed to be. "If you have any more trouble, track me down. You don't want to mess with these power cables by yourself. They've got a lot of juice in them."

"Thanks," I said to Ernie as he scurried off to help the next vendor whose lights were on the blink.

• • •

Tiffany showed up at my table a few minutes after the show opened.

"Jax, I think we need to have another chat," she said.

"Can this wait? I am trying to run a business here. I sell beads when I sit at this table. When I'm not at this table, I don't sell as much."

"Hey!" said Tessa, offended that I would make it sound like she was slacking off.

Tiffany leaned across my table, pressing her hands down on a tray of beads covered with spiky dots. It couldn't have been comfortable.

"Did you know Carl Shulman?"

"Who?"

"Don't play dumb with me. The security guard who was found dead in the stairwell."

"No."

"Did you kill him?" she asked.

"No." Seriously, this woman needed lessons on how to ask good questions. Maybe she could learn something from watching Jeopardy. "I mean really, Tiffany. I have no idea who this guy was. I've never met him, and I don't even know what he looks like. I don't know why anyone would kill him." I was getting pretty tired of these chats. I just wanted to get out of here—all the way out of here, like back to Seattle.

"You know, Jax, I think you're hiding something from me. And you know what that means?"

"No idea."

"It means I've got a new pair of bracelets for you. Ones with a nice silver chain," the detective said, pressing her wrists together, miming what I'd look like with handcuffs on.

There was a woman with a baby stroller standing behind Tiffany, trying to get her hands on the earrings I was selling. The detective was blocking her way.

"If you can please step aside, I have a customer who would like to buy something." Tiffany was not going to take me to the police station on suspicion of murder. Not if I could help it.

"I'll chat with you again soon," said the detective as she squeezed her way past the stroller.

"These earrings are sooo fun. I want this pair. Ohhh, and this pair too. And maybe these," said the woman with the baby.

"Wonderful, I'll wrap those up."

• • •

"Jax, I don't like it when you're so quiet," said Tessa. "It usually means you've got plans to do something you shouldn't be doing."

I wanted to solve the mysteries of the dead bead diva *and* the dead security guard, if for no other reason than to stop the constant requests for chats with Tiffany.

"Sal said Saundra lived nearby. I'm thinking about going out to her house."

"You're just going to drive out to Saundra's house?"

"Yes. Maybe I can find a clue."

"No, Jax, don't do it. There's nothing you can learn there," Tessa said.

"If I can find something, *anything*, that would keep Tiffany from booking me on suspicion of murder, I'd like to find it."

"*Che casino*," Tessa muttered, knowing it was too late to stop me.

"I need to see Saundra's house and her studio, maybe talk with her brother. It might be that someone broke into Saundra's studio and stole her beads. Maybe that's why that young woman had them. I don't know what I'll find, but I'm hoping there's something out there that can help us bring this whole mess to a close."

"Then I'm coming with you. Maybe you'll stay out of trouble if I come along," Tessa said. Usually Tessa tagging along meant I still got in trouble, just less of it.

"Tessa, you need to stay here," I told her. "Who will work at my booth? Val can come with me instead."

"You're going to take Val?"

"I can't have her work in the booth. Val doesn't know the first thing about beads," I reminded Tessa. "And her math skills are pretty questionable. How would she be able to calculate sales tax?"

"There's no sales tax in Oregon," said Tessa, being annoyingly accurate and practical. "Val can work your table. I'm sure of it."

"Tessa, please. Be my best friend and work at my table. I trust you, and I promise I'll be careful. According to Sal, Saundra's brother lives at her house, and maybe Val will be able to sweet talk him in some way so we can find out what we need to know." I'd made up my mind. It was either take Val, or go alone.

Customers continued to stream into the bazaar and among them was Val, several inches taller than everyone else, thanks to her sky-high footwear. She bustled toward us with a cardboard tray holding three white and green Starbucks cups.

"One for each of us. A large latte for Jax and a small espresso for Tessa," Val said. "And one for me."

"What is that thing?" I asked, eyeing Val's fancy whipped-cream-topped slushie with sprinkles on top.

"It's a Venti caramel macchiato, with extra caramel, extra whipped cream, and extra sprinkles," said Val, pulling her drink out of the tray, taking a sip, and leaving a smudge of red lipstick on the straw.

Val took a step toward us with the drink tray and stumbled as her high heel caught on the bedspread I'd used as a makeshift table covering.

The drinks toppled over sideways, their lids popping off as they did. I was hit with a dark brown tidal wave.

The coffee soaked my shirt, which had gone from white to brown, and almost as bad, there was none left for me to drink.

"I'm so sorry," Val said. "We need to get you upstairs and changed."

"Tessa, can you run the booth?" I asked.

"Yes." Tessa looked at me with squinty eyes and arms crossed, and not from a lack of coffee. "*Che casino,*" she muttered again.

"You know Val and I are going to do more than just change my clothes, don't you?"

"Yes." There was a sigh behind that word. "Don't take The Ladybug if you're trying to be discreet."

I agreed with Tessa. A bright red VW bug isn't the best option when you're flying under the radar.

"Come on, Val," I said. "We have an adventure awaiting us."

"Oh goodie!" Val said.

TWENTY-SEVEN

"WHAT ARE WE GOING TO DO? Some reconnaissance? Some honey trapping? Some kind of super-sleuthy thing?" asked Val. "Do we need a gun? Because I didn't bring mine."

Val has a gun?

"Don't get so excited. We're only going to Saundra's house. We'll check her studio to see if we can find anything out that will help us learn what happened to her, maybe talk with her brother, and find out who's stealing either her beads or her designs."

"Got it. We're looking for clues."

"Yes, we're looking for clues." I was already beginning to regret bringing Val with me.

"We'll take Firefly," Val said.

"I've always wondered, why is your car called Firefly?"

"It's a space ship. Oh, and also the name of a TV show. Actually, the name of the ship is Serenity, but I like Firefly better. It's such a shame they cancelled the series…" She trailed off, seeing my confusion. I shouldn't have asked.

Val's car, unlike her, was subtle. She owned a 2005 gray Honda Civic, which reminded me of the old car I'd traded in a few years back when I left Miami behind, along with Jerry and my dead-end job. Val folded herself into the car. It was far too small for a woman of her stature, especially when she fluffed up her hair to full height. She pulled off her high heels and flung them into the back seat. There were a dozen other pairs that had met with the same fate back there.

We turned up Skyline Boulevard, while I used the GPS on my now fully-charged cell phone to give us directions. As we headed off into the hills, the road narrowed and went from two lanes to one lane, and then to gravel.

"Stop the car," I said.

"Here? This can't be right," Val said, confused. "I thought Saundra was supposed to be some famous bead artist." A small shingled house sat at the end of a dirt path, edged by a rickety split-rail fence.

"This is the address I saw on her contract," I said, double-checking the GPS route to make sure it hadn't sent us to the wrong location. "This is the place. Let's go check it out."

Val pulled herself out of the car and stretched her legs. She really did need a bigger vehicle. She fished out a pair of heels from the back seat and was ready to go. We headed down the path toward the house. Off in the distance, brown and white cows ambled around in a fenced hilltop field.

Val picked her way down the unpaved trail in her tall shoes, leaving pockmarks in the dirt as she walked. "It's just plain spooky around here."

"Sal said Saundra had a brother who lives with her. I'm not sure if we'll find him home or not."

"I don't like it here, I don't like it at all," Val said, pulling a bottle of perfume out of her purse. From a tree branch above us, three crows cawed as we continued walking toward the house.

"Don't spray any more of this," I said, grabbing the bottle from her. "Why does the label say Chanel No. 6?"

"It's better than Chanel No. 5. The guy I met on the sidewalk—"

"You bought perfume on the street?"

"It was a good deal. I'm just a working girl—" She grabbed the bottle from me and tucked it back in her purse.

"You don't even know what's in that—"

I heard the click of metal on metal and fell silent. I glanced at Val. She heard it, too. The crows took flight, sweeping low before heading toward the hills.

"Do not move," I mouthed to her.

"What?" Val said, far too loudly.

"Put your hands up," a man said.

I put my hands above my head and turned slowly.

He looked exactly like Saundra. Except he was a man wearing a green John Deere hat. And he was alive. And he was holding a twelve-gauge shotgun, pointed right at us.

TWENTY-EIGHT

"THE COPS HAVE ALREADY BEEN here to tell me about my sister," the man said. "So what are you two doing here?"

"I was a friend of Saundra's," I said. "I wanted to come out and make sure you were okay." This was a fib, but I didn't want him to think we were random strangers who were trying to break into his sister's house.

"Can I turn around?" Val asked.

"Just keep your hands up," he shouted.

Val turned slowly. Doing as she was told, she kept her hands in the air.

"Hi there," Val said, once she was turned toward the man. "My name's Val. What's yours, honey?"

The man looked at Val, his eyes blinking rapidly. Who was this woman who was introducing herself to him, as if there was no gun between them? He pushed back his cap to get a good look at us.

"And this is Jax," Val continued. "Say 'hi,' Jax."

The man looked from Val to me.

"Hi," I said, showing him my biggest smile. "Can we put our hands down? Please?"

"Please, honey, we aren't going to cause any trouble, we promise," Val said.

"Okay, okay. But no sudden moves," the man replied.

"Now, I still didn't get your name," said Val as she took her hands from above her head and put them on her ample hips.

"It's Bruce. Now listen, just because I let you put your hands down, that doesn't mean we can be all buddy-buddy, you know?"

"Nice to meet you, Bruce," said Val, plunging on ahead, ignoring the fact that the man still seemed ready to fire his gun at any moment. "Now, we came out here because we knew Saundra. And were heartbroken when we heard that she'd died. We just wanted to see how you're doing."

Val could charm just about anyone. Nothing she had just said was true, but that didn't matter. If she could stop Bruce from filling us with buckshot, that would be a step in the right direction.

"That's real nice of you. Real nice. But I've got to be careful. A famous bead artist like Sandy—I mean Saundra, that's what you'd call her—dies, I think about all the people who'll be coming here to try and steal her stuff. You know, like all the artists whose work gets more valuable after they die."

I'd seen Tessa do that very thing when she bought the stack of books from Miles with the hope of turning a quick profit on the autographed books of the now-deceased artist.

"I'm sorry. Saundra was your sister, right?" I asked.

"Yup, my big sister," he said, finally dropping the shotgun to his side.

"You poor thing," said Val, stepping closer to Bruce. Immediately, he was back on his guard, but Val was too fast. She closed in on him with a big hug.

Bruce went limp, his plaid shirt coming untucked from the force of Val's hug. She had a way of doing that to people. When Val finally released her hold on Bruce, we sat down on a bench near the side of the house.

"You two didn't just come out here to see me, did ya?"

"We wanted to talk with you about how Saundra died," I said.

"Yeah, I can't believe she cracked her head open like that."

"That's the thing; we don't think that's how she died."

"Then what happened?" Bruce asked.

"We're still trying to figure that out, but from the way the police are acting, it seems that someone might have killed her," I said. "That's the reason we're here. We wanted to see her house and studio. We thought it might help us figure out what happened, maybe give us some clue about who would have had something to gain by Saundra dying."

"There's not much to see. That's her house. You can go on in and take a look around, but I'm coming with you. I'm still not sure that you aren't both just treasure hunters here to steal from a famous dead artist."

Bruce brought us into the tiny two-bedroom house. Saundra's bedroom was full of all the beautiful clothes that she was well-known for: silken skirts, finely woven shawls, long delicate dusters, and miles of scarves. The other bedroom was Saundra's bead studio. It was empty, except for a clean white table, a torch, a few thin rods of glass, and a camera.

"That's odd," I said.

"I agree," said Val. "This is the tidiest studio I've ever seen." Val has seen my perpetually messy workshop plenty of times. "I mean, really, wow, I had no idea a studio could be like this. I can even see the countertops."

"The only places I've seen that were this sterile were the clean-rooms in the Clorox labs," I said.

My studio is always chaotic, and this was at the opposite end of the spectrum. This space was too immaculate for any real creativity to occur. It was as if Saundra cleaned up before leaving for the week-end. Could she have known she was never coming back?

"Did you see your sister work in her studio much?"

"I live up the hill at the ranch. It was just her in this valley. She liked having her privacy, and I don't think she liked the cattle much. I'm not sure what all happened down here."

"Did she have people over to visit?"

"Oh, lots of people visited. She did have this one friend, always dressed like a clown. You know—covered in polka dots."

"Wendy," Val said. Two points to Val for being a super-sleuth.

"And then some wimpy dude, I think his name was Miles."

"Yes, Miles, we know him. He's Saundra's assistant."

"Then there was a young woman. She didn't have much to say. I'd see her at the gate. She'd show up with a big stack of cigar boxes, and I'd help her get them in and out of her truck. Always a little skittish, like some of my calves."

"Do you know anything about her? Her name?"

"I'm not sure if she was a bead lady or not. She, uh, didn't really look like some of the other bead ladies I've met."

Could that be the mystery woman who I'd run into last night? I wasn't sure if I'd ever be able to find her because she certainly didn't want to be found.

"'Course, there were lots of others, too. Hard to tell some of them apart," Bruce said. "Sorry, I can't be much more of a help."

"That's okay, we understand," said Val, patting Bruce on the shoulder as we stood on the front porch of Saundra's house. Val truly could do almost anything, and people just let her.

"It's been real nice talking to you ladies. I hope you figure out what happened to my sister. She's all I had, other than the cows. I've got to get up there and get them corralled," Bruce said, looking up the hill.

"We promise if we learn anything about your sister, we'll be in touch with you."

Bruce set down the shotgun on his pickup truck. It was piled with all sorts of ranching tools, various prods and hooks, and branding irons.

Val and I walked down the dusty path to her car. I could see the footprints of the people who had passed this way: boot prints from the police officers who came to tell Bruce the bad news about his sister, pockmarks from Val's heels, many other prints and scuffs, and some small tire tracks as well.

• • •

Val and I climbed into the car. She took off her high heels, and once again flung them in the back seat, then clicked on the radio. There was no reception out here in the boondocks. I reached over and turned it off.

"You know how Bruce asked us how Saundra died?"

Val nodded.

"How *did* she die? I was the only one who saw Saundra after she died, other than the police and the coroner. What did they see that I didn't, that would make them believe she was murdered?"

"I saw this one episode of *Star Trek*, where Mr. Spock, being so logical—"

"Shhh, Val, you can tell me about that later," I said, not wanting to hear anything more about her sci-fi obsession. "If I knew how Saundra died, maybe that would lead us to the killer."

As we drove away, we could see Bruce standing in the gravel road, very alone.

TWENTY-NINE

WHEN VAL AND I ENTERED the lobby of the hotel, the first person we saw was Tiffany. The detective looked like she was waiting for someone. It turned out she was. She was waiting for me.

"Jax. I've been looking all over the place for you." I wasn't sure I wanted Tiffany to know we'd been out to Saundra's house, and I hoped Val wouldn't volunteer that information.

Val reached out her hand to shake with Tiffany. It was the oddest thing. These two women were cut from the same cloth. More than once I'd gotten them confused with each other, at least briefly. They did have the same taste in footwear, after all.

"Val, this is Detective Houston," I said.

"You can call me Tiffany," the detective said.

"And Detective Houston, this is Val."

"You can call me Val," she said, with an unexpected edge in her voice. Knowing Val as well as I did, I could tell something was wrong.

"Why don't you come with me? We can have a little chat," Tiffany said, as she guided me into the small conference room that she'd turned into her interrogation room.

Val stood in the conference room doorway, trying to figure out whether she should come in.

"Can Val join us? She's really good with understanding human nature," I said, although sometimes she had a little too much to say on the subject.

"Too true. You see, I'm a hair stylist, and I've heard it all. So many crazy stories..." Val settled into the chair next to me without waiting for the detective's invitation.

"Val? Let's just move on. I'm sure the detective has some questions for me," I said, patting her knee.

"Do you know what the person who trashed your room last night was looking for?"

"No idea," I said.

"Ryan gave you your belongings back this morning?" Tiffany asked.

"Yes, he did."

"And did you notice anything missing?"

"No. I didn't look closely, but from what I saw, everything was there." The only thing missing at this point was my sanity.

"What do you think the connection is between the deaths of Saundra Jameson and security guard Carl Shulman, and your room being trashed?"

"I'm not sure there is one." I was relaxing a little bit. She was asking a good question. "I can't think of a common denominator, other than all three events happened here at the hotel. I can't imagine why anyone would kill the security guard. Maybe he saw something happen when Saundra was murdered, and the killer was trying to cover his tracks."

"That idea has some merit," said Tiffany. "But how does your room fit into this?"

"I don't know how any of this fits together. I'm sorry. I wish I did," I said. "I don't know who would trash my room." Other than the maid who had interrupted me when I was breaking into someone else's room.

Tiffany's phone rang, and she answered it. While listening to the caller, she opened the email program on her iPad. "I already saw that report. Thanks for sending it. Interesting to see the C.O.D.," she said to the person on the phone. She listened for a reply, then hung up.

"What have you girls been up to?" Tiffany asked, changing gears.

"Oh, just a little shopping," Val said. Thank goodness Val was on my wavelength. Although there was really no reason to lie about where we were today, I didn't feel like volunteering that information.

"Funny, that's not what I heard," Tiffany said with a tense smile. "I heard you went off to Saundra's house. Doing some snooping around without me, Jax?"

"Uh…" I said, completely unclear about what I should say next, and doing it ineloquently. "Uh…" I said again.

"Jax, I thought we were a team on this. Now you've brought your pal Val into the situation. I told you very specifically that you were not to speak with other people about this case. You're going to land in jail for obstructing a police investigation."

"I, I—" I continued in my inarticulate way. Val sat next to me, glowering at Tiffany, hands clasped together in front of her. Her long, red nails tightly gripped the back of her opposite hand.

"We did a little shopping, and while we were in the neighborhood, we thought we'd stop by Saundra's house," I said. This, of course, was complete nonsense, since there were no shopping malls within miles of Saundra's house.

Tiffany let us off the hook, now that I'd spilled the beans. Or is that *beads*?

"And did you learn anything at Ms. Jameson's?"

"Not really. We met her brother."

"Yes, he was nice," Val said. "Though I think he could use a makeover—the tractor company logo baseball hat is not a good look for anyone older than fourteen. And that red and orange plaid shirt, he could use an updated pattern in a more flattering color."

Tiffany stopped taking notes on her iPad when Val starting talking about Bruce's makeover. The detective sat impatiently, tapping her red nails—cut to a much more practical length than Val's—on the table, waiting for Val to stop. But Val was not getting the hint. The detective's phone rang.

"I'll be back in a minute," Tiffany said, stepping out of the conference room, leaving her iPad behind. We watched her walk away, her patent leather shoes flashing their red soles with each step she took.

"When the detective was on the phone, she said something about an interesting C.O.D. What do you think that's about?" I asked.

"Cash on Delivery?"

"No, I'm thinking Cause of Death."

Val and I both looked over at the iPad.

"Are you thinking what I'm thinking?" Val asked.

"If you're thinking that there's an autopsy report we want to see on that tablet, then yes, we're thinking the same thing."

"Quick, give it to me," said Val.

"I'm not sure—"

"I want to see that iPad," she insisted, reaching across the table and pulling it toward us. Val pressed the screen with one of her knuckles, and the screen blinked to life.

PASSWORD:

"Oh, crap, Val. We need a password. Okay, let's try this," I said, grabbing the tablet.

I typed *password* on the screen, trying the most obvious choice.

Invalid password. Three more attempts.

I tried another common password: *abc123*

Invalid password. Two more attempts.

"Jax, let me try, okay?" Val pulled the iPad in front of her and concentrated. She placed one hand on the edge of the screen and put her other hand to her temple.

"I don't think the Vulcan Mind Meld works on iPads." In fact, I didn't think it ever worked, except on *Star Trek*. And if you were Mr. Spock. I ran to the door to keep an eye out for Tiffany. I didn't want her to find us doing any digital breaking and entering.

"I'm getting something," Val said, her hand still at her temple.

"Hurry, she'll be back any second."

Val typed *gucci*

Invalid password. One more attempt.

"Of course not Gucci. It would *not* be Gucci," Val said, her hand back at her temple.

"Last chance, then I don't know what happens—the thing locks up for some period of time or explodes or something," I said.

Louboutin, Val typed.

Access granted.

"Wow! It worked," I said, astounded.

"Wow, that Vulcan Mind Meld thing really does work," Val said, impressed with herself.

"What's a Louboutin?" I asked.

"Oh Jax, you should know that. You're a woman. You should know more about shoes than just high tops and clogs. Louboutins are shoes with red soles. She's wearing a pair today."

"So maybe it's not the Vulcan Mind Meld?"

"It worked. All I'm saying is that we were locked out, and now we're in, so you better see what you can find out before Tiffany comes back," Val said, trading places with me at the door. "And you can thank me later."

"Let me see, what do we have here?" I tapped on a file called "Medical Examiner's Report."

Subject, female 59 years old, history of heart arrhythmia, cause of death cardiac arrest subsequent to electrocution. A single oval 1.5 inch by 2.5 inch contusion with charring indicative of high voltage contact at L4, base of spine. Additional insubstantial contusions and abrasions, seventeen mirror fragments ranging in size from .25 to 1.5 inches, superficial, excised posterior aspect of cranium and trunk...

I also found the medical examiner's report for Carl Shulman.

Subject, male, 48 years old, cause of death, blunt force trauma, distinctly square contusion measuring 1 inch by 1 inch, anterior aspect of cranium...

"I think she's coming, we've got to stop," said Val.

"Just one more thing here I want to see," I said, as I took a quick peek at a page called "Reports from Security Guard Ryan Shaw."

Val grabbed the iPad, pressed the lock icon, wiped off our fingerprints with the edge of her sweater and slid the tablet back across the table.

The iPad skidded to a halt, just as Tiffany returned to the room. "Sorry, ladies, I've got to dash." Tiffany looked down at us, as we sat there looking like two innocent school girls. She grabbed the iPad and was gone in a flash.

"Thanks. You saved me."

"That's right. I saved you. You and me, Jax. Not you and *Tiffany*."

"You don't like her? I thought you'd be the best of friends. You're so, so…"

"What? Don't say we're the same, because we *are not* anything at all alike."

"Really? Because it seems to me that you have a lot in common. You like the same clothes, the same nail polish, the same—"

"Look, you told me this more than once. You have to look past what's on the outside and look at what's on the inside." I told her this when I was giving her advice on choosing a boyfriend—that she should look for one who isn't just pretty packaging.

"I said that. And you went out and found Rudy, the ugliest, meanest-looking guy I've ever met."

"Who, first, is not my boyfriend, as I have tried to point out to you more than once. And, second, looks fantastic after I fixed him up."

"All true," I agreed. Rudy was a gruff painting contractor we met a few months back who had transformed into a good-looking man, thanks to Val. He turned out to be a nice guy as well.

"Tiffany and I may look the same on the outside, but on the inside, she is a snake in the grass. Not to be trusted."

I wanted to trust Tiffany—trust that she wouldn't haul me away to jail on suspicion of murder or for obstructing her investigation.

"She's just a little different than I'd expect a detective to be, starting with the name Tiffany. But how could her parents have known she was going to be a homicide detective when she grew up?"

"Seriously, Jax, I grew up around girls like her, back when I did beauty pageants—"

"You competed in pageants?"

"Of course I did. I grew up on a farm in Iowa—I was Miss Junior Pork Chop Queen. I got to be in a parade on the Fourth of July, sitting on a float, waving to my adoring fans. They made me a scepter out of a livestock prod," Val said, reminiscing. "I learned to love hairstyling during those pageants. I can tell you, girls like her, they're all nice to your face, but behind your back, you can't trust them."

"Livestock prod? Like a cattle prod?"

"I told you this whole story about me being a queen, and the float, and the adoring fans, and all you can say to me is 'livestock prod'?"

"Did you ever use a cattle prod? Could you kill someone with one?" I asked.

"Probably not. My uncle Herbie used to zap Herbie Jr. with one."

"Why did he do that?"

"I think Herbie was a family name," Val replied, missing my point.

"No, I mean, why did he zap his son?"

"Oh, just for fun."

"For fun—seriously?"

"It never seemed to hurt Herbie Jr. that much. He was never really right in the head, but Herbie Sr. wasn't either. It ran in the family, I guess. Herbie Jr. was strong and healthy. But, Jax! Saundra had that lack-of-rhythm thing in her heart, right?"

"Arrhythmia. If she had a heart problem, then I wonder if a cattle prod could have killed her," I said. "That's what it seems like the coroner was saying."

"It really could be true," agreed Val. "What now? Do you have another mission for me?"

"Why don't you go up to the room? Maybe you can check on Gumdrop," I said.

"You're right. He might be lonely." Gummie did not get lonely, but it was a good idea for someone to check on him, since he was in unfamiliar territory.

"I'm going to go back to my table. I'm sure I've left Tessa alone too long," I said.

I found Tessa where I'd left her, sitting at my booth. The crowds had thinned, and Tessa was staring off into space.

"Hey, there. Did you make me a million dollars selling beads this afternoon?"

"No."

"Half a million?"

"Sorry. No." Tessa was not in a happy place.

"Is this because I left you at the booth for so long, or because chaos continues at your house, or because you're hungry?"

"All of the above."

"Cheer up, Tessa, because today is almost over, and then we can have some drinks, and dinner, and then more drinks."

"What did you learn on your adventure with Val?" Tessa asked.

"I learned that Saundra keeps a *very* tidy studio. What would you say if I told you someone's studio was so pristine that it basically didn't have anything in it?"

"Saundra's studio was clean?"

"Immaculate. So clean you could see the countertops."

"That *is* mysterious. Art is messy. Never trust an artist with a clean studio, that's what I say."

"Then Saundra was the least-trustworthy artist ever," I said. "Also, I learned Saundra didn't die from falling and cracking her head open on the mirror."

"What?"

"She was electrocuted."

"She was electrocuted after she fell down? That doesn't make much sense."

"I think it may be that she was electrocuted and then fell down." Tessa stared at me in disbelief.

"I got a peek at the coroner's report," I said.

"I don't want to know how you were able to do that."

"It said that Saundra had a big oval burn at the base of her spine. Someone electrocuted her."

"What could have caused an injury like that?"

"All Val and I could think of was a cattle prod," I said.

"That can't be right," she said.

"I know it seems highly unlikely—but not impossible. Val said that if someone with a weak heart was zapped with a cattle prod, they could die."

"Since when is Val an expert on electricity, or electrocution, or—"

"And the autopsy said that Saundra had a heart condition," I said.

"But who would have a cattle prod?" she asked.

"Saundra's brother. He's a rancher, he'd have one," I said, but as soon as I said it, I realized there was someone else I knew who had a cattle prod.

"Are you thinking what I'm thinking?" Tessa asked.

"Vance."

THIRTY

"**WE HAVE TWO PEOPLE** who have the same weapon, but seriously, who could walk around a bead bazaar with a cattle prod and go unnoticed?" Tessa asked. "And neither of those men have a motive."

"No motive that we know of. Saundra's brother, Bruce, seemed paranoid and trigger-happy. He almost shot Val and me when we showed up at his sister's house unannounced. And Vance, with all of that scary gear in his room, who knows how violent he could be."

"And remember, someone vandalized our room—that could have been Vance."

"I know, but just because the guy uses Vandal for his studio name doesn't mean he's an *actual* vandal."

Luke strutted past on the way to his booth. The long oilskin coat he was wearing fluttered as he walked.

"What about Luke? He's got a long coat on, long enough to hide a cattle prod," I said. "He certainly had a reason to kill Saundra," I added. "She cost him a lot of money when she was a no-show at the class she was supposed teach."

"I don't know, Jax. It seems like there are almost as many suspects as people at this show."

"I'm pretty sure it's not Sal. He seemed to have worked out his problems with Saundra before the show started," I said.

"Miles?"

"Saundra didn't treat him well. But he seems too wimpy to kill someone. Although he might be able to fit a cattle prod into his ukulele case," I said.

"He plays a ukulele—how could he possibly be a murderer?" asked Tessa as she stepped around to the front of the table to neaten things up.

"Beep beep!" Wendy zipped by Tessa, nearly running her over. "You shouldn't be standing in the middle of the aisle."

"You shouldn't be driving your scooter over the speed limit," Tessa replied. Too late—Wendy was gone.

Tessa tugged on one of Vance's table lights to adjust it. It flickered and went out.

"I'm sorry. I think I might have unplugged the light," Tessa said.

I crawled under the table and looked at the plug. It was still connected to the socket of the beat-up power box, pieces of black tape holding together a cable that snaked toward another booth down the aisle.

"I figured it out," I said to Tessa, pulling myself back into a chair.

"Well, the light's still not working, so I'm not sure you did," Tessa said.

"I think I know what killed Saundra, and it wasn't a cattle prod."

"What was it then? The hand of God?" Tessa made the sign of the cross, just in case she shouldn't be joking about God. "A lightning bolt? Static electricity?"

"Remember when Ernie was here fixing the power? He said the cables had a lot of *juice* running through them."

"They hook into the main power supply for the hotel, I think," Tessa said.

"I think someone jammed one of these frayed cables into Saundra's back and let a million volts hit her spinal column," I said.

"The hotel was having all sorts of electrical problems on Preview Night. Maybe Saundra's murderer caused the blackout when he—"

"Or she—"

"—zapped her."

"The killer must have been near Saundra when the blackout started happening. Like Miles, who was working in her booth," I said.

"You were practically right next to her, Jax. No wonder the detective thinks you're the prime suspect," Tessa said. "But you're not the killer, right?"

"Geez. No, Tessa, you *know* it's not me."

"I know, I know, but it has to be someone here, and so far, I don't think we've found a single person who is a reasonable suspect, or could even point us in the right direction."

"I wish I could find the mystery bead seller. She's involved in Saundra's death somehow," I said. "It's too bad the Saturday Market is only open on Saturdays. I'm certainly not going to wait around in Portland for another week to find her."

"But it *is* open today. It's called the Saturday Market, but it's really the weekend market," Tessa said. She must have known that by admitting this, she was doomed to stay working at my booth while I went to the market in search of a woman with green hair.

"Tessa?"

"How can I help you?" Tessa said, but not to me. She was greeting a customer who was approaching my table. She glanced over her shoulder and mouthed the words, "Good luck!"

• • •

When I got to the elevator, Vance was waiting there along with several other hotel guests. Two elevators arrived at the same time and when the doors opened, all of us were hit with the smell of Val's Chanel No. 6. Vance and I stepped into one of the elevators together. It still seemed mysteriously cold, although maybe not as cold as it had been previously. Maybe Val's perfume actually did keep away ghosts.

"Hi, Vance. Thanks for the lights," I said as the elevator doors clunked shut. I was nervous being in the elevator with him. He seemed harmless enough, but after seeing all the kinky gear in his room, plus the possibility that he'd vandalized my room, I was worried about what he was capable of doing, especially in this confined space.

"You're welcome," Vance said, fumbling with his glasses, which were completely broken in two. "Do you have any duct tape on you?" he asked.

"No, but Tessa has some tools and glue up in the room. I'm headed up there now if you want to come along." Since Val would be in our room, at least I knew I wouldn't be alone with him. Vance looked up at me. His cheek was bruised, red and purple.

"What happened to your face? Did someone hit you?"

"Oh, well, that. Yeah, I was afraid someone might see that," Vance said, looking back down at his broken glasses.

"Vance, who hit you?" I asked, as I took the pieces of his glasses from him and tried to figure out how we'd be able to put them back together.

"Can I trust you?" Vance asked.

"Of course," I said. It was nice that he trusted me enough to fix his glasses.

He reached over and pushed the emergency stop button on the elevator, and it screeched to a halt between floors.

"Geez! Vance! What's up with you? Are you crazy? Start the elevator up—now."

"Jax, I need to talk with you. It's about Lin. She's a maniac. Ever since I started buying all those props for the photo shoots, she's really gotten into the part. At night she puts on those clothes and gets out the leather cuffs. It scares me. A lot."

"Did she hit you, Vance?" I asked. It was completely ridiculous that the tiny, demure Lin could do anything to hurt big, soft Vance. "Vance, are you listening to me? Did she hurt you?"

"It's just that she kind of kicked me in the head while I was lying down."

"No!"

"Yes, like I told you, she's been trying out all sorts of things. The whip…"

"Did she use the cattle prod on you? Don't tell me she used the cattle prod."

"That thing? We bought it from a theater company—it has nothing inside it to shock anyone. I'm glad, though, because I really wouldn't want to get electrocuted."

Vance's cattle prod didn't work. It seemed unlikely that Bruce would have driven all the way from the country to zap the life out of his sister in front of dozens of bead ladies, when he easily could have killed her at her house. Unless someone else at the bead bazaar owned a cattle prod, which I highly doubted, then Saundra Jameson was electrocuted using a giant electrical power supply cord.

"How can I help you?" I asked.

"Fixing my glasses would be a good start." Vance pressed the emergency stop button again, and we continued all the way up to the tenth floor.

THIRTY-ONE

I KNOCKED ON THE DOOR.

"Who is it?" asked Val, a note of suspicion in her voice.

"Val, it's me. Open up."

"Jax, is that you?"

"Of course it is. Let me in."

"But how do I know it's you?"

"Because if you don't let me in I'm going to...to...Gah! I don't know what I'm going to do. Just open the door, will you?"

"What's the secret password?"

"We don't have a secret password."

"Okay, good job. The answer to the question about a password was that we don't have a password, so you passed the test."

"Val..." I said, with an exasperated sigh, pressing my head against the doorjamb.

Val opened the door and let me in, Vance in tow.

"Well, who do we have here?" Val said, looking at Vance with a gleam in her eye. She was targeting him as her next makeover project, or victim, depending upon your point of view.

"Val, this is Vance."

Vance shook her hand, still holding his broken glasses.

"Are those your glasses?" Val asked.

"They're broken, and Jax thought she might be able to fix them." I found Tessa's jewelry kit, and with a little glue and sterling wire, I pieced the glasses back together. He would still need to get some new frames, and if Val got her way, she'd be helping him make that decision, among others, from here on out. I placed the glasses on Vance's nose, and he looked better already.

"Now, what have you got going on there?" Val asked, pointing at the large bruise on Vance's cheek. "Oh, never mind. It doesn't matter what it is at this point. Let's just fix it with some makeup."

"I don't think I should stay. I—my wife—she's a little jealous. I wouldn't want her to find me here."

"Here's the number of my salon," Val said, pressing her business card into Vance's hand. "Call me next time you're in Seattle, and I can reboot your whole look."

And with that, Vance bolted out the door.

"Reboot?"

"I'm getting into this hi-tech thing…now that I've become a computer hacker," Val said.

"Just because you guessed the password on someone's iPad doesn't make you a computer genius."

"Pffft." Val blew me a small raspberry.

"Can you go down and help Tessa in my booth?" I asked Val.

"No, honey, I can't," Val said, plumping her red hair in her reflection from the gold-leafed mirror behind the sofa. "I promised Luke I'd help him in his booth. I hope he does that thing to my neck when he puts on a necklace. So sexy," she said, running her own hands around her throat and imagining they were Luke's.

"When you've been with Luke, did you two ever talk about Saundra?"

"He mentioned something about Saundra giving him some private lessons. She owed him for some reason. But really, Luke and I never do that much talking, if you know what I mean," she said, nodding and smiling at me.

"I don't want to hear—"

"Because we're working in his—"

"Yuck. I don't want to hear what you're working in—"

"We're working in his *booth*. Such a dirty mind you have," Val said, scolding me.

"I can't believe you'd leave me to work at someone else's booth."

"You have Tessa. You don't need me," Val said, turning from side to side to make sure she looked terrific from every angle.

"You're perfect," I assured her, as Val put on an extra coat of lipstick, smacking her lips together.

"Val? I need your help."

"What is it, darling?"

"Can you make me look, uh, like you?"

"I've been waiting for this moment since I met you," Val said, hugging me.

"This wouldn't be a permanent change, just a temporary thing. I need to look different for a little while so someone won't recognize me." The mystery bead seller wouldn't want to talk with me after I'd chased her through the streets of Portland. I hoped a disguise might help, so I could learn something from her before she realized who I was.

"That's a start. Maybe you'll love your makeover so much, you'll decide you want to dress fabulously every day."

In the bedroom, Val made a beeline for her overnight bag, and pulled out a dress—a tiny dress.

"Do you actually wear that thing?"

"Sure, but I usually wear it with some leggings because it's pretty short, even for me." Val was five inches taller than I was, so something that was too short on her might be a reasonable length on me.

"Wow, Val, that's the first time I've ever heard you say something was too short."

"I think it will be faboo on you."

"But, the color, seriously. I don't think pink with black dots is my style."

I was beginning to regret asking for Val's help.

"Maybe I'll just wear this," I said. I was comfortable in jeans and a red T-shirt, and a coordinating necklace, of course.

Val gave me a withering look. "Yes, but then you'll look like you always do. Aren't you trying to look different?"

"Pink with black dots it is," I said. If I was going to disguise myself, I might as well go all the way. "You know who would like this? Wendy," I said.

"Wendy the Polka-Dot Princess?"

"That girl just loves her spots. Every bead she makes—covered in dots. Everything she wears is covered in dots as well. She must have been a Dalmatian in a previous life."

"Oh, yes, I saw her table yesterday. All those dots were making me go cross-eyed," Val said.

"She's okay, and she's been making beads for a long time. Funny, she never seemed to have progressed from making spotted beads. She's really good at making them, though."

"She could change things up, don't you think, with her outfits and her beads," Val said, adding a wide black belt to my costume. "She could wear something a little less wild—something neutral."

It was hard to believe Val would want someone to be subtler because if one word described Val, it was "over-the-top." That's more than one word, but it does describe her accurately.

"You need shoes," Val said, looking at my feet with a grimace.

"Sorry. I've got these—" I said, looking down at my red leather clogs.

"And those icky green sneakers you were wearing yesterday," Val said, handing me a pair of patent leather sling-back heels. "Put these on."

"There's no way those will fit me. Your feet are much larger than mine," I protested, handing them back as quickly as she gave them to me.

"They're sling-backs. They have this little strap that's adjustable," Val said, pushing me into a seated position, kneeling and jamming a shoe on one of my feet, then buckling it tight.

"Ouch!"

Val put the other shoe on my other foot and stood up to admire my new shoes. She pulled me up so I could try them out.

"What do you think?" Val asked.

They were a little tall for me, but I admit they made me look—and feel—cute.

"I like the shoes," I said. "I don't know if I can walk in them, but I like them."

"You know, honey, if you can't walk in them, you can lie down in them, and you know—"

"Val, I don't want to talk about what I could do in bed with shoes on."

"Because that hunky Ryan guy, oh, or the sexy Detective Zach—"

"Get your mind out of the gutter. Let's focus here," I said, sitting down on the edge of the bed. I was feeling a little tippy on the narrow heels.

"And now, your face," Val said, grabbing a small suitcase and putting it on the bed. She pulled up a chair in front of me and started sorting through the case.

"Ah, okay, foundation, powder, eye liner, eye shadow, mascara, and lipstick," Val said, taking inventory of all the products she was going to need to work her magic.

"Please be gentle, I'm not used to wearing a ton of makeup," I said.

"You don't want to be recognized, do you?" Val's eyes gleamed in a way I'd never seen before. "Don't worry, I'll make you look gorgeous. No one will recognize you."

"I'm not sure that was a compliment," I said, kicking her with her own shoe.

"Sorry, honey. I'm glad you trust me."

"And you've got ten minutes."

Val went straight to work, with only a few mutterings to me to hold still, blot my lips, and finally to close my eyes. She puffed my face with powder and ran her hands across my forehead and cheeks one last time.

"Ooh-la-la," said Val. I kept my eyes shut tight. "Jax, that means you're supposed to open your eyes."

I slowly opened them, worried about what I'd see in the mirror Val was holding. She had actually made me look like a different woman. My skin tone was so smooth and even, not a single freckle showing. I had about two pounds of blush on my cheeks. The electric blue eye shadow was a little much, but it definitely made me look like *not me*, which was what I was after.

"Wow! What a terrific job you did," I said, admiring her handiwork in the mirror.

"You're gorgeous," Val replied.

I couldn't call myself beautiful, but I did look different, and that's what I needed if I wanted to be unrecognizable to the young woman I was searching for at the market. If I toned down the makeup about ninety percent, it would have been the perfect look for me.

"Do you have anything for my hair?" I asked Val.

"Oh, yes! You're going to let me style your hair too?" she asked. She opened a tiger-striped tote and started pulling out an arsenal of hair care products. "Of course, you don't have much to work with," she complained, looking at my tousled mess of light brown hair. I'd been wearing it short for about six months, ever since I'd singed off my bangs in a studio accident involving a scorching hot kiln.

"Val, I just need some gel or something," I said.

"Gel is so '90s. You need some wax," Val said, scooping some sticky purple goo from a container.

"No, Val. Please…" But it was too late. She rubbed her hands together, and then ran them through my hair. I closed my eyes and let her do what she wanted. There was no restraining her.

"Ooh-la-la," Val said, and I knew it was time to look.

I opened my eyes and looked in the mirror. Val had worked her magic. My hair looked cute and coifed, definitely not my usual style.

"Wait, I have one more thing that will help you," Val said, reaching up and removing a hair clip from her head. Attached to the clip was a puff of hair. "I sometimes need some extra fullness here at the crown of my head."

Val headed toward me, holding the fluffy hairpiece.

"Come on, Jax. It's so cute. It's called a wiglet. Kind of like a tribble."

"What's a tribble?" Whatever it was I didn't want it.

"They're cute little aliens on *Star Trek*—"

"No, Val, I am not putting a tiny alien on my head," I said, backing away from her.

"It's not a real alien, darling. Those TV shows, they're fake," Val said. It scared me to think Val felt she needed to explain that to me. Val definitely had the advantage—she knew how to walk in high heels. She cornered me.

"Now hold still," Val said, clipping the vile thing to the top of my head and pulling my hair up around it. Val held me back at an arm's length. "Let me get a good look at you. Hmmm. It's not really the right color. Let's just—"

"Stop. No more! Tessa's watching my booth right now, and soon she'll get tired of sitting there, because she's missing her chance to shop. I've got to get to the market and get back as soon as possible before she explodes," I said as I grabbed my handbag and wobbled out the door. I hoped I wouldn't see anyone I knew as I crossed the lobby.

THIRTY-TWO

THE LAST TIME I WENT to the Saturday Market I walked, and it took longer than I'd anticipated. This time, I was driving. Walking would be difficult, at best, in Val's clothes and shoes. If I walked, the worst-case scenario was that I'd get picked up by the cops on suspicion of selling more than beads. Val could pull off the sexy look—me, I just looked like someone had dressed me up and put me out on the street. Which, in fact, was what happened.

When I got in The Ladybug, I looked in the rearview mirror and nearly screamed. Actually, I really did scream. I ripped the tribble off my head and jammed it in my handbag. I was not going to wear that thing out in public. I put on a black felt hat that was in the back seat. It didn't go with the rest of the outfit, but it was the best I could do. If I'd had a knit cap, I would have fit in much better, since it was Portland, after all.

As I drove, I remembered what Val had said about Luke—that Saundra had offered him private lessons. I assumed that meant that Saundra decided to make up the money he lost by giving him a one-on-one class or two. If this was true, then Luke wouldn't have wanted to kill Saundra. Plus, Luke's booth was not near Saundra's, which would have made it difficult for him to zap her from behind.

And even though he wore a coat that could have concealed a cattle prod, it was clear that it was not the most likely murder weapon at this point.

I parked a block from the market and adjusted all my body parts to make sure nothing had shifted in the dress on the drive over. Then I checked my lipstick in The Ladybug's side mirror before heading off down the street. It was difficult to swing my hips, as Val would have done, especially when I was wearing someone else's shoes that were two sizes too big. I decided it was better to concentrate on simply walking from the car to the market without falling down and breaking my neck.

The market was bustling when I arrived. I scanned the tables as I walked from booth to booth. Handmade jewelry that ran the gamut from elegant to funky filled the first few booths, but there were no glass beads. Stalls with veggies, candles, and hand-knit sweaters followed. Vendors displayed handmade ceramics, jams and jellies, and T-shirts with clever sayings. Finally, I saw a booth with a display of glass beads in cigar boxes. I casually sauntered over to it.

A woman sat at the table, her hair tucked up inside a knit cap—so much for identifying this woman by her hair color. A small hand-made sign on the table read: *Beads by Brynne.* That name didn't ring a bell. Keeping my eyes down, I focused on the beads and hoped the woman wouldn't recognize me. The person I was looking for only got a glimpse of me the night before. I hoped the clothes and makeup Val put on me would be enough to make me unrecognizable and that I'd have a few minutes to talk with her without her bolting, as she had done the night before. I looked in the boxes. They were full of Saundra's beads. Either stolen or knock-offs, it was hard to tell.

This was the mystery bead seller I'd been searching for. Brynne wasn't trying to engage me, her potential customer, but was instead focused on her phone. I thought I'd start out slow, with some basic questions to see what I might learn from her without arousing her suspicion.

"These beads are really unique. Did you make them?" I asked, picking up a Fenestra bead, another design I recognized as Saundra's, with tiny window-like portals that you could look into to see the bead's colorful center.

"They're handmade from Italian glass. I create all these beads using a torch." She was talking, and she didn't recognize me. This was a start.

"I make glass beads, too," I said. "But mine aren't as nice as these."

"Cool, thanks." She returned to looking at her phone.

"Did you take classes around here?"

"I learned on my own from books and YouTube. Oh, and then I learned a lot working with this guy, Miles."

Miles. He was the connection. Somehow Miles linked this woman to Saundra, but I didn't know how or why.

"Did you ever meet him?" she asked. "He's a beadmaker. Pretty cool guy. I met him at the Urban Sea Monkeys concert. They're an obscure band with a retro-folk-synth sound—you've probably never heard of them. I listened to them back before anyone else did. But now, they've just sold out to the commercial market." No wonder she liked Miles. They shared that hipster desire to listen only to esoteric bands and to bad-mouth musicians who achieved any level of commercial success.

Should I tell her I knew Miles? Should I tell her my name?

"No, sorry, I haven't met him," I lied.

"You want to buy a bead, or what?" she said, looking up at me.

As we made eye contact, she jumped up from her stool and backed away from me. "Hey, you're the lady who was following me last night. Who are you, an undercover cop?"

Oh no! My cover was blown. She'd recognized me. So much for Val's costume. Maybe I should have kept the wiglet clipped to the top of my head.

"I'm not a cop." Brynne was looking from side to side, trying to figure out what her escape options were. "Look, you can't run away and leave your beads behind. Just sit still and talk with me."

"I didn't do anything wrong," Brynne said. "And by the way, that's a really sucky disguise you have on." I decided I'd let the insult slide.

"I need your help. Someone killed Saundra Jameson."

"Look, I barely even knew that bit—"

"Your beads, they look just like some of Saundra's."

"Yeah, I wasn't supposed to sell them at the market. They were supposed to be hers, but they didn't turn out so well, so I didn't sell them to Miles."

"You were selling beads to Miles?"

"Yeah, he'd give me the designs, and I'd make them," Brynne said. "It was an easy way to make bank each month."

Saundra wasn't making her own beads? What a crazy idea: A bead-maker who didn't make beads. I knew she was able to make them, having seen her demo a few months back at Tessa's studio. Now I knew why Saundra's studio was so neat—nothing was ever made there.

I also understood now what Saundra's brother, Bruce, meant about the people who came to visit Saundra. There was a woman who didn't look like the other bead ladies—because she had green hair.

"Do you know why anyone would want to harm Saundra?"

"I'll tell you this, I made a lot of money in this deal. I wouldn't kill her. I didn't like her, but I liked her money."

"What can you tell me about Miles?"

Brynne started closing up the cigar boxes that held her beads, clipping the lid of each box in place with its square metal clasp. I was running out of time.

"Saundra didn't treat Miles very well, but he kind of needed her. He told me once he couldn't get another job. Not sure why."

"Can I buy a few of your beads?" I asked. "How much for these three?" I might need them later, although I wasn't sure why.

I paid Brynne, and she placed my beads into a little woven bag, then put away the cigar boxes in her backpack. She folded up the tablecloth she'd been using and stuffed it in as well.

"Hope you catch your killer," Brynne said, slinging her backpack onto one shoulder.

"Hey Brynne, any way I can get in touch with you?" I called to her as she left.

She glanced back at me. Without a reply, she slipped into the crowd and was gone.

THIRTY-THREE

WHEN I GOT BACK to The Red Rose Hotel, I went straight up to our room. I didn't want anyone seeing me in this getup. As I slid the key card into the lock, I heard a loud howl from the other side of the door.

Gumdrop was unhappy. He was not going to be happy until he was home. I opened the door slowly. My cat was sitting on the plush white sofa, now covered in long gray fur. He let loose another long howl. His green eyes were slits in his otherwise fluffy face, and his front claws were extended, gripping the sofa cushion. I sat down on the sofa next to Gummie and gave him some long strokes down his back, and a vigorous scratch under his chin. He kneaded his paws in my lap.

"Ouch! I'm going to clip your nails when I get home. You scratched Ryan yesterday, you know," I said to the cat. He looked up at me with his grumpy eyes and let loose a plaintive, "Yellloooo."

I pulled off Val's clothes and slid into my own jeans and back into the red ribbed T-shirt I'd had on earlier. Val's makeup remover was on the bathroom counter, and I used it to take off the makeup she'd slathered on me. I slipped on my red clogs and was down at the bead bazaar in a matter of minutes. Tessa was working at my table, as she had been for much of the last few days. She was writing up a sale when I arrived.

"And here are your beads," Tessa said with a big smile. "Thanks for your purchase." I sat down behind the table with Tessa. She handed me the receipt book, and I flipped through the pages.

"Looks like sales have picked up a little," I said. Things had been slow earlier in the day. Buyers were now zipping through the bazaar one last time to pick up any items they'd been thinking about, but hadn't purchased earlier.

"I'm really happy for you Jax, you deserve it. I didn't do much. People just love your beads."

"Thanks, Tessa. You're not angry I've been gone for so long?"

"I'm okay. Glad I could help my best friend make a ton of money. You're buying me dinner this week, of course, to make up for all my hard work," Tessa said.

"Absolutely. Any restaurant you want. You want me to take you to Ray's Boathouse?" That was one of Tessa's favorite places, near her house on the Shilshole Bay. We'd spent many afternoons drinking white wine on the upstairs deck, watching the sun sink over Puget Sound.

"That sounds great," Tessa said, giving me a big hug. "Did you find the mystery bead seller?"

"As a matter of fact, I did. Her name's Brynne," I said. "And after talking with her, I have some serious questions for Miles."

"What does he have to do with all of this?"

"It looks like Miles asked Brynne to make beads for Saundra. He'd bring her designs, and she'd make the beads. At some point in the process, Miles would pay Brynne and deliver the beads to Saundra."

"So you've uncovered a pretty unethical way of doing business. You don't think it's illegal, do you?" asked Tessa.

"No, as long as the bead designs belong to Saundra, she could do what she wanted with them, including have someone else make them."

"Really? Because that just doesn't seem right," she said.

"What I want to know is how Saundra's murder fits into a scheme in which Brynne, a beadmaker no one knows, makes beads for one of the most well-known glass bead artists," I said.

"If someone murdered Saundra to hide this scheme, could they also be after Miles or Brynne?"

"If someone was after Brynne, they'd have trouble finding her." She didn't want to be found, but I wasn't sure why.

And what about Miles? Was he in danger? Or was Miles a mastermind who had created a plot that had ultimately led to Saundra's death? After all, Miles had been near Saundra when she died. Why Miles would want to kill Saundra was another question entirely, other than the fact that she treated him badly, which didn't seem like a reasonable motive for murder.

Time to track down Miles, and, to use Tiffany's expression, *have a chat*.

THIRTY-FOUR

MILES WASN'T AT MINNIE'S BOOTH, where he'd been most of the weekend. So much for him helping me at my table.

"If you see Miles, send him over, okay?" I asked Tessa as she sped away to shop one last time, worried, I was sure, that if she didn't leave now, I'd ask her to man (woman?) the booth for another hour or two.

"Can I get those extra books back from you?" Miles asked when he showed up at my table a few minutes later.

"Did Tessa tell you I wanted to see you?"

"I haven't seen her. Look, I just need to get those books. A bead store is coming by the loading dock to pick them up. I promise I'll come right back." He reached under the table and grabbed the box of books.

"Miles. Sit." Miles perched on the chair next to me, the books in his lap. "Are you okay? I've been a little worried about you."

"I'm fine," said Miles. He wasn't giving me anything to go on.

"Nothing's bothering you?"

"No, I'm cool," Miles said, adjusting the vintage watch on his wrist.

"And how's Minnie?"

"She's fine too." I needed some lessons on how to interrogate someone. I wasn't sure what questions to ask Miles, but I didn't want to alarm him, or have him think I was accusing him of any-thing. Asking questions like "Did you kill Saundra?" and "Do you know who did?" were right out of Tiffany's playbook, not mine.

One of Minnie's bead trays crashed to the floor, and Miles looked over as she scrambled around picking up beads. Miles looked at me with sad puppy eyes. He reminded me of Stanley the Basset hound, minus the bloodshot eyes and droopy lids.

"Go on, go help her. I'm fine," I said. "Here, take this envelope back to Minnie. It's everything I borrowed this weekend, plus twenty dollars to pay her for the supplies I used." There weren't going to be many more sales this weekend. I held on to a partially used receipt book, in case there were some last minute buyers.

"I promise we can talk a little later," Miles said, dashing off to help his new girlfriend, the manila envelope resting on top of the box of Saundra's *Celestial Bead Designs* books.

I recalled what I'd found in the envelope the day Miles gave it to me. There were detailed sketches of a design that looked like one of Saundra's beads, and several pages of notes, written in a round-lettered handwriting that many girls in middle school tried to perfect. Saundra had told me she was unveiling new designs in the *Celestial Bead Designs* book at Bead Fun. If that was true, why did Minnie have Saundra's notes and drawings? Had Minnie stolen them from Saundra?

Tessa had given me Saundra's book, and I found it on the floor under my tote bag. It had a big, gorgeous image of the new Cosmos bead design on the cover. I wondered if this book would ever be worth much. I wasn't sure if I could even bear to keep it, since I'd just as soon forget about this weekend. I opened the cover of the book. Saundra's spidery signature was scrawled across the first page. Ostentatious until the end.

The signature looked nothing like the writing on the note pages I'd seen in Minnie's envelope. Saundra's writing was jagged and sweeping. The pages of notes had looping round letters. If that wasn't Saundra's writing on those note pages, whose was it? Minnie's? And if they were Minnie's notes, what did that mean?

I looked over at Minnie's booth. A sheet had been thrown over the top of her display. She was gone, and so was Miles. Minnie had left her beads and her show gear on her table, so I knew she'd be back, but I couldn't wait until then. I was worried about Miles—had he gotten caught up in something he couldn't handle?

Miles said he was headed to the loading dock, and it was possible that Minnie was with him. Adriana was wandering from table to table, making some last minute purchases, perhaps trying to see if any vendors were willing to give her some end-of-show discounts.

"Adriana!" I shouted to her. "Can you help me for a few minutes?"

"Sure. No problem," Adriana said, sliding behind my table. "What do I need to do?"

"Just sit here and make sure no one steals anything. If a customer wants to buy something, just have them pay in cash. And if anything complicated comes up, call me. Thanks!"

I trotted down the aisle, dodging dazed customers who were wrapping up their weekend of frenzied bead buying. At the back of the ballroom, I passed the utility room, then sprinted down an industrial gray hallway. I skidded around the corner and smacked into the side of an orange forklift at the back of a large warehouse.

THIRTY-FIVE

FROM MY HIDING PLACE behind the forklift, I could hear Minnie shouting. Her words, echoing inside the cavernous warehouse, were punctuated by the sound of a thrown object meeting its target, followed by a small squeaking sound.

"YOU (thunk squeak) GAVE (thunk squeak) THOSE (thunk squeak) PAPERS (thunk squeak) to JAX (a final thunk, but no squeak)." Minnie must've missed Miles that time. "I was in the clear. Nobody needed to know what happened."

I peered around the front of the forklift. Miles was standing at the edge of the loading dock, his hands protecting his head. Minnie was ten feet away with a half-dozen books in her hands and an empty box next to her. Books surrounded Miles, covers open and pages torn. Minnie had been throwing Saundra's books at him, and some of them had caused him damage, judging by the red welts on his face and arms. I couldn't stand seeing poor Miles abused like this. Against my better judgment, I decided to rescue him.

"Cut it out, Minnie. You have no right to treat Miles that way," I said as I ran to his side at the edge of the loading dock.

"No right? No right! I most certainly have a right. He worked for that monster. She stole my design and put it on the cover of her book. How could you let her do that, huh, Miles? How could you?"

"I swear I didn't know it was your design. Saundra said she invented it, and I trusted her. She was my mentor, why would I think she was lying?" said Miles.

"The Cosmos design was *mine*," Minnie said, throwing another book at Miles. He dodged it, and it went flying over the edge of the dock. "I showed her some pages of notes—these notes—six months ago at a bead retreat." There were loose pages of drawings and notes on the floor that I recognized as the ones I had just given back to Miles. Minnie stomped on them with her floral army boots. "She said the design was okay, but she didn't think it would sell very well. I was discouraged and didn't make any more after that." Minnie started to deflate as she heard herself admit her own failure in giving up so easily. Miles stood a little taller, precariously close to the edge of the dock, kicking books off his chukka boots.

"When I saw the pages of notes that Jax had, I recognized your writing. I watched you write receipts for three days, so I know how you write, like some of the girls I knew in junior high, the loopy words with hearts dotting the i's," Miles said.

"I don't dot my i's with hearts," Minnie said, dropping a pile of books on the floor for emphasis. The noise reverberated through the warehouse. "At least not very often."

"When I brought those pages back to you, I didn't really understand what they meant. But I get it now, those were the drawings of your design," Miles said.

"Cosmos was my design, and Saundra stole it. When I saw the beads on the cover of her book, I just lost it. How could she do that to me? Why didn't she even talk with me about how she wanted to make something similar?"

"You could have made your designs anyway," I said. "She wasn't the only one who was allowed to make beads that look like a starry night sky."

"And have everyone say my work was soooo derivative of Saundra's? That I was copying *her*, when really it was the other way around? That woman was vile and deserved to die."

"You killed Saundra?" asked Miles.

"No! What? No, I didn't kill her. Seriously, I wanted to kill her, but really, I wouldn't do that. It wouldn't be right," Minnie said.

"Why does it matter that I had the notes?" I asked. "Saundra was dead, and if you didn't kill her, the notes don't matter."

"But they do matter. I didn't want anything to connect me to Saundra—I didn't want to be accused of killing her because she'd stolen my design."

"After I told you I had some of your papers at the Cheesecake Factory, did you realize what I had and try to get them back?" I asked.

"I did, but obviously, I wasn't successful. There was always a security guard watching the door to the ballroom, so I couldn't check to see if you had my papers in your booth. The only place I could look was in your room."

"Did you trash my room looking for your notes?" I asked.

"When I got to your room last night, someone had already been there. There was a security guard standing at the open door. His face was red, his nose looked like a...a...strawberry. The place was upside down—but I didn't do it. When I saw the guard, I just kept walking down the hall," Minnie said. She had described Carl Shulman, the guard with the ruddy face and the bulbous nose.

"You'll have to tell that story to the police. I'm sure they'll want to hear it, especially since that security guard was found dead in a stairwell last night," I said.

"I don't know what you're talking about! But I know this—I can't go to jail. Do you know how it would be in there?"

"I imagine it would be pretty awful," I said.

"They wouldn't serve kale—or quinoa. I'd have to wear an orange jumpsuit, which would be fine, except everyone else would be wearing one too. There'd be arts and crafts using yarn and wooden beads. Trust me, I know how it is..."

"You've been in prison," I realized. "And you don't want to go back."

"My parole officer has been looking for me. I really don't want the police to track me down—I'll end up back in prison." Minnie rushed toward me, hands out, trying to push me off the end of the dock. "Let me show you how serious I am about you keeping your mouth shut."

And while a drop of four feet wouldn't kill me, I didn't want to crack my head open. I'd had enough of people doing that this weekend, and for the rest of my life.

"Jax!" Tessa called out to me from across warehouse.

The cavalry had arrived.

THIRTY-SIX

WITH HER GUN DRAWN, Detective Tiffany Houston swung into the warehouse and ran toward the edge of the loading dock where I stood with Minnie and Miles. Tessa, Val, and Ryan were right behind the detective. "Everyone, I want your hands where I can see them," she shouted.

Minnie spun around to face the detective. We all put our hands up.

"Jax, you can put your hands down," said Tiffany, through gritted teeth.

I put them down and moved away from Minnie and Miles. If Tiffany was going to shoot, I didn't want to be in the line of fire.

"Minnie Dean, you are under arrest for the murder of Saundra Jameson," Tiffany said.

"But—I—I swear it wasn't me," Minnie said. "I'm a vegetarian, I can't even think about killing an animal. How can you think I could kill a person?"

"I ran your name through our police database, and it appears that you have quite a colorful history—don't you, Minnie? Sergeant Anderson, your parole officer, has been trying to find you," said the detective. "And Miles, you've had a bit of a checkered past as well, haven't you?"

Miles stood at the edge of the dock, still holding his hands above his head.

"It wasn't my fault," Miles said. "And it happened a long time ago."

"Come on, Miles, you need to tell us what you know," I said.

"Jax, let me clear something up with you," said Tiffany. "There is no *us*. There is just *me*. Thanks for playing along, though."

"I told you she couldn't be trusted," Val whispered in my ear.

We all stood silently, waiting. Miles looked over at me, and I nodded slightly, encouraging him to talk.

"I was at U of O for a while, an art major. I got involved in some student protests, mostly about budget cuts and tuition hikes. I would bring my ukulele, and we'd sing protest songs during the rallies. I was good at playing 'The Times They Are A-Changin'' in a completely non-ironic way.

"One time when we were out in front of the administration building, a bunch of campus police officers came by, and they started harassing us, roughing us up a little bit. A big cop moved toward me, and someone pushed me from behind. The sign I was holding bashed the cop in the face. They cuffed me and took me away. A felony attack on an officer. After that, I couldn't get a job. Any job that required a background check, which is pretty much any job, I would fail because of the arrest. But Saundra, she said she'd take me, as long as I kept her secrets. And I did."

"And what secrets would those be?" Tiffany asked.

"Let me see if I can explain it," I offered. "Miles, if I get something wrong, you can jump in. Saundra wasn't making her own beads. Someone named Brynne made them."

Miles looked at me, wide-eyed and open-mouthed. "How did you—"

"I found her at the Saturday Market. She was selling beads that she shouldn't have been selling. I haven't figured out why this was going on, but it most certainly was. And I have the evidence here to prove it," I said, pulling the beads I'd bought from Brynne out of my pocket. "Miles, you introduced Brynne to Saundra. Brynne was making Saundra's beads, and it was a good financial arrangement for Brynne, and you too, I imagine. Have you got anything to add, Miles?"

"That's not illegal," Miles objected.

"No, but it certainly does make me wonder what other secrets there were between you and Saundra. What would make you want to kill her?"

"Are you kidding me? I didn't kill her. I worked for her. If she died, I would have no job."

"But you set up transactions between Saundra and Brynne. You sold beads that were not made by Saundra and claimed that they were hers," I said.

"They were her designs. She could do whatever she wanted with them."

"In the case of the Cosmos bead design, it didn't belong to Saundra, it was Minnie's," I pointed out. "That makes Minnie seem awfully guilty. She certainly had a motive, and she did have a table near Saundra that would have placed her close enough to hit Saundra with a thousand volts straight into her spine."

"I had no idea that Minnie killed Saundra. That was a terrible thing to do, Minnie," Miles said, standing up to his full height.

"I didn't kill Saundra!" Minnie yelled.

"But what about Miles? How did he fit into your plan?" I asked Minnie.

"What plan? I didn't have a plan. I met Miles, we had a little sex. And I mean a little," Minnie said, with a disappointed glare at Miles. "He worked in my booth—he was useful. Then I realized Mister Brilliant here," nodding at Miles, "had gone and given you the drawings of *my* beads and basically framed me for the murder of *The Great Saundra Jameson*."

"Giving those papers to Jax along with the rest of the supplies was an accident. I was trying to be nice. You should try that some time," said Miles. I could see that Miles's and Minnie's relationship, or whatever it was, was on the rocks.

"I think it's time to go, Minnie," said Tiffany, clipping a single handcuff onto her wrist.

Miles blew out a sigh of relief, like he thought Tiffany was going to let him go.

"And you're coming, too," the detective said to Miles, grabbing his wrist and cuffing him to Minnie.

THIRTY-SEVEN

"BETTER LUCK NEXT TIME," Tiffany said to Ryan, patting his face sharply, then pulling Miles and Minnie across the warehouse and down the hall.

"I hate that woman," I said. "Val, you were right. She wasn't what she appeared to be. And definitely *not* a team player."

"You've got to look at the inside of a person. That's what I always say," Val said.

"No, Val, that's what *I* always say."

Tessa, Val, and I had a group hug, and Ryan hung back, not knowing what to do.

"Ryan, get over here, you need a hug too," I said, squeezing him tight, and then reaching up, grabbing his sweet face, and giving him a kiss.

Tessa and Val stood there looking at Ryan and me, mouths agape.

"Get a room, you two," said Val. "This is a hotel, after all."

Tessa's phone buzzed, and she answered.

"Oh, no. Oh, no, no, no," Tessa said. There was a new crisis at home.

Ryan took me aside. "You go and take care of your friends. Please don't leave without saying good-bye."

"Don't worry, I'll find you," I said over my shoulder, as I walked down the hall flanked by Tessa and Val.

Tessa covered the phone with her hand. "It's Ashley. She says that Izzy shaved the hair off one side of her head. Joey's locked himself in his room with Stanley—" Tessa stopped in the middle of her sentence. "Wait a minute. What is Stanley doing at my house?"

Val didn't have a chance to explain.

"Ashley, put your dad on the phone!" Tessa demanded. Her conversation with Craig continued in half-Italian and half-English, until finally she hung up the phone, tossed it dramatically into her purse, and zipped it shut. Tessa was giving her phone, and all the people on it, a big time-out.

"I think you both should take off," I said.

"I want to be here for you, but I'm worried about how out of control things have gotten at home," Tessa said.

"Your family needs you," I told her. "Val, can you give Tessa a ride back up to Seattle? And take Gummie with you. He's miserable."

"I'm so sorry I brought Gumdrop. I just didn't know what else to do," Val said. "Don't you need us here?"

"There are only a couple hours left of the sale, then I need to get everything packed up. I won't be far behind you. Gummie needs to get home as much as Tessa does."

"I suppose so. But what if Bruno comes back and threatens me?" Val asked.

"Pick up Stanley from Tessa's," I advised. Tessa glowered at me. She clearly didn't like the thought of Stanley at her house, adding to the mess and destruction that was occurring at the moment. "And if Bruno comes back, you just tell him you've got your attack dog ready and that you'll unleash him if Bruno doesn't leave immediately."

"Stanley doesn't look ferocious," Val said.

"Do you know that if you say 'speak,' Stanley will bark?" I'd discovered this last month, but had yet to use it to scare someone. "Just get him to bark through the door at Bruno, and I expect he won't stay on your doorstep for long."

"What a super idea. I knew there was a good reason to keep Stanley. I always thought he was a guy magnet, which he is. But I also like that he can be a guy repellent," Val said.

"All right, you two. Get packed up and get out of here. Adriana's watching my booth, and I need to get back there before the show closes," I told them. "Are you two going to be okay heading home without me? Do you think you can handle Gumdrop?"

"We'll be fine once we're on the road, and I can put on some classical music," Val said.

Tessa gave Val a confused look.

"I'll explain it on the drive home," Val said. "If we get hungry, we can stop at Taco Bell. And I'll drop you off at your house. That way I can pick up Stan—"

"Val, maybe you should be going now." I didn't think it was a good idea to bring up Stanley again.

THIRTY-EIGHT

I HOPED I HADN'T left Adriana alone too long in the ballroom.

When I finally got back to my table, she was holding court, telling stories about the good old days in the bead world to a rapt audience of other vendors. Virtually all the customers had gone home, as often happens in the last hour of a sale like this.

Finally, we heard the announcement we were waiting for. "Ladies and gentlemen, the Bead Fun sale is now closed. Please make your final purchases and proceed to the exit."

I pulled out my cash box and flipped through the money I'd collected and the receipts I'd written from my sales this weekend. I'd done well. Very well. Deciding to treat myself to a small splurge, I walked to Indigo's table. Her canvas-lined trays were full of nature-inspired sculptural beads. I especially loved the autumn-colored leaves. There were only a few of those left.

"Is there still time for me to buy one of your beads?" I asked Indigo.

"Sure, but don't you want to trade instead?"

I'd seen many beadmakers trading beads at events, but I'd never done it myself. I didn't want to trade with Indigo, though; I knew she needed the money.

"I'd love to trade sometime, but for now, I'd like to buy this one," I said, plucking a sage green and rusty orange leaf-shaped bead from her tray, and placing the money for it in her hand.

"Thanks," Indigo said, shoving the money in the pocket of her batik skirt, then carefully wrapping my bead in wrinkled—clearly re-used—blue tissue paper and tying it with a piece of jute cord. "Thank you, and namaste."

"To you, too," I said awkwardly, not sure what else I was supposed to say or do. "See you at the next bazaar."

I headed back to my table to pack up. I pulled out all the junk that had accumulated under the table and threw it away. I stacked my bead trays in Tessa's tote. As carefully as possible, I unplugged the lights from the power supply and wrapped the cord around the base of each fixture.

Vance was at his booth taking his displays apart and packing up. Lin was nowhere in sight.

"Thanks for the lights," I said when I arrived at his table. "They really helped."

"You're welcome," Vance replied. "And thanks for fixing my glasses and letting me confide in you."

"No problem. I don't see Lin—what happened to her?"

"She's over there with The Twins. Lin decided that she's going to give up all her scary costumes. She knew she was getting carried away, but she couldn't help herself when all that kinky stuff was around."

"What's that got to do with The Twins?"

"She's selling them most of our more outrageous costumes—turns out they love that stuff, not for, you know, in the bedroom, but just as fashion statements," Vance said. "They said something about how their inner soul needed to be echoed in their outer carapace. But I didn't really understand what that meant." I expected no one, not even The Twins, knew. "And I'm going to give up the name Vandal. Once I talked with some people about my beads, things got better, and I actually sold a lot of inventory this weekend. I realized I didn't need to hide behind Vandal anymore. I could just be plain old Vance Dalton, and that would be fine."

"I'm so glad to hear that. Your work is very special, and so are you. See you at the next bazaar?"

"See you there," Vance said, adjusting the newly-fixed frames of his glasses.

"And if you come up to Seattle, let Val know you're coming, and she can help you pick out some new eyeglasses."

I spotted Lin coming toward us, a wad of cash in her hand. She gave us a big thumbs-up and a smile. Vance seemed pleased. With Lin's clothing sale, they'd definitely made enough money to make this show profitable for them. I hoped he and Lin would have a better relationship going forward.

Back at my table, I neatly organized all the items we had borrowed from the hotel room. I folded the sheets and comforter, and put the Bibles and dishes on top of the tidy stack of linens. Dropping them off at the front desk, I told the clerk they had been removed from room 611, and requested that they not charge my room for the missing items.

I ran into Sal on the way back to my table.

"Hey, I got your things. The ones the cops took. They're all packed up in a box in the utility room. I could show you where it is, and you know, maybe we could spend some quiet time back there."

"No way, Sal."

"You're right. There's not much privacy, what with Ernie coming and going. Meet me in my RV in an hour?"

"Not on your life."

"Your loss," Sal said.

My phone started playing its little calypso tune.

"Val? You're home already?" I asked.

"It's a short drive, honey, and the way I like to drive Firefly, it's super-short. Gumdrop wanted to get home, poor thing, his howling was lots worse this time. It must've been all the catnip that made it easier on him on our way down. He didn't have any on the way home."

"Okay, thanks for letting me know you're home. And Stanley?"

"Stanley wasn't ready to come home yet."

Tessa must have been overjoyed.

"Any sign of Bruno?"

"No, and I'm glad. I'm so over him. You know, he cheated on me at least twice. Then he comes to my house and accuses me of cheating. How hypothetical is that?"

"Hypocritical," I said. Val completely ignored my correction and kept on talking.

"And the thing is, I should have known after he cheated on me the first time that he was no good. You know, if someone cheats once, they'll probably cheat again."

"Val. You're brilliant."

"I am?"

"You are, Val. You most definitely are."

"Okay, gotta run. I've got this cute guy coming over later."

"What about Luke?"

"You're not going to believe this! When I was working at his booth, I watched him do that sexy neck thing to every woman who came by."

"Tessa and I warned you. It's his sales technique."

"Well! I was pretty upset about it! I mean, really, I thought I was special!"

"You are special. You just need to meet the right man. Tell me about the guy who's coming over later?"

"I met him at Taco Bell."

"You're going to go out with a guy who works at Taco Bell?"

"No, silly, he's a massage therapist who was buying some Mexican food for dinner. I told him to come on over, and I'd cook him a nice meal—better than Taco Bell, and then he promised me a nice—"

"Bye." I hung up before I heard anything more about what the massage therapist was going to do to her.

If someone cheats once, they'll probably cheat again.

I knew Saundra had stolen a design from Minnie—one design, for the Cosmos bead. But what about all the other designs? Did the bead diva cheat to get those as well? And who would know about the other people involved in this scheme?

Miles would know. He would know who Saundra was stealing designs from. But Miles was going to be hard to question, now that he'd been cuffed and taken away. At least Tiffany had gotten to cuff someone this weekend, and I was glad it wasn't me.

If Miles couldn't help me, then who could?

THIRTY-NINE

SAUNDRA'S BROTHER SAID many people had come and gone from Saundra's house over the years. If I knew who had been to her house, it might be easier to figure out who she had stolen designs from. On the dirt path leading up to Saundra's house, I'd seen foot-prints and small tire tracks. I'd seen tracks like that before. Ryan had dodged them as he looked for Gumdrop in my thrashed room.

I called Ryan. "Can you get me into my old room?"

"I could, but I don't think the people who are staying in it would be very happy about that," Ryan said.

"Dammit! I wanted to see the vacuum cleaner tread marks across the carpet."

"Are you still trying to figure out what happened to Saundra?" Ryan asked. "Because that is over, Jax. Time to let it go."

"Something isn't right. Those tracks—remember how you avoided stepping on the vacuum cleaner tracks in my room? My room had been cleaned earlier in the day, and someone trashed our room that night. The maid wouldn't have entered a room that had been turned upside down, and she wouldn't have come in at night after having cleaned it in the morning."

"I know how we can find out when the maid was in your room."
I heard Ryan on his radio talking with the front desk, and then back
to me he said, "The maid's on the sixth floor. Let's go up and talk
with her. Meet you there in a couple of minutes."

I pushed my tote of beads under the table and left the ballroom to
meet Ryan. He was waiting for me when the elevator doors opened.
The maid was at the end of the hall, near my old room.

"You!" said the maid when she saw me, scowling with her dark
eyebrows pulled in tight.

"She's okay, Consuela. She's trying to help me," Ryan said.
Consuela alternated between smiling at Ryan and glaring at me.

"When was the last time you cleaned this room?" Ryan asked the
maid. Consuela checked her clipboard.

"Saturday morning and this morning before the new customers,
Mr. Ryan," Consuela said.

"Not Saturday night?" I asked.

"No!" said the maid, clearly still angry with me.

"Consuela, thank you so much, and I'm sorry about the other day
when you found me trying to get into that room on the fifth floor."
I pressed twenty dollars into her hand. "Here's a tip for doing such
a good job cleaning my room." Consuela continued to glare at me,
even with a twenty-dollar bill in her hand.

"Thanks, Consuela," Ryan said.

"Thank you, Mr. Ryan," Consuela said.

"I've got to go," I said as I dashed for the stairwell.

There was another way to make tracks like we'd seen in my room.

FORTY

THOSE HADN'T BEEN vacuum tracks; they were from a scooter. Why would Wendy tear my room apart? I had no idea what she might have wanted, or even if she had found it. Even if Wendy had been in my room, that didn't mean she had killed Saundra. But why was she in my room, if not to cover her tracks? In the end, she hadn't done a good job in covering her figurative tracks or her literal ones.

When I got to Wendy's booth, it was empty. Everything had been packed up and taken away. Now that she was gone, there was no way of getting my questions answered. Tiffany already had her suspects in custody, and I doubted she would see pursuing Wendy's breaking and entering as anything more than a waste of time.

The only thing left to do was to pack my gear into The Ladybug and get out of there, and the sooner, the better. As I headed through the ballroom, the last few vendors were shutting down their booths. I didn't have much more to do and was glad Sal had told me where my impounded items could be found. I passed through the door at the back of the ballroom and took the corridor to the utility room. The room was long and narrow, not much wider than the hallway.

Running the length of one side were stacks of boxes and cleaning supplies, while the other side was a rat's nest of power supplies and cables. While I was poking around looking for my box, there was a soft electrical purr behind me. I turned around to see what it was.

"Oh, Wendy, hi. I didn't hear you come in. I'm so glad I found you before you left."

"Yes, I'm pretty quiet, other than the sound of my scooter. And it's pretty quiet back here, too—I bet no one can hear us out in the ballroom." She was making the hairs stand up on my arms.

Wendy got off the scooter and lumbered toward me. The red and yellow bullseye dots on her black shirt looked like dozens of bloodshot eyes staring at me. I needed to distract Wendy and slip by her so I could get help. Jewelry is always a good distraction.

"Oh, Wendy, how pretty. You've got a bracelet with a Cosmos bead in it," I said, admiring the beaded cuff on her wrist. "Saundra had one just like it. I noticed it when I first met her, before…you know, before…"

"Before she died?"

"Yes, before her tragic accident." I wasn't going to let her know that it was murder, though I suspected that she already knew that. "The clasp had come undone, and I caught her bracelet before it fell. Is your clasp the same? Does it stay together well?"

She held out her hand to show me the bracelet, and I caught a glimpse of a red streak across the inside of her wrist. Wendy pulled her arm away from me.

Something was wrong. Very, very wrong.

Ryan had a similar mark on his wrist. Caused by a furious cat. A cat who was in my room when someone ripped it apart looking for something.

Now I was certain that Wendy had trashed my room. I didn't know why, and I really didn't want to find out. I'd had enough of being an amateur sleuth—I'd let Tiffany, or some other homicide detective, figure it out. Right now I needed to get out of here. There wasn't much space in the narrow room to slip by Wendy, and her scooter was blocking the doorway behind her. It would be impossible to get past those two obstacles. I hoped I could simply talk my way out of this, and find Tiffany or Ryan.

"Jax, you and your friend Tessa. You two, you've known each other a long time?" Wendy asked.

"Most of our lives," I replied.

"Don't you at times just want to cut her out of your life? To reveal to the world what an awful person she is?"

"No, I don't, because she isn't an awful person. I trust her with my life."

"Hard to believe," Wendy said, plodding slowly away from her scooter, pressing me back farther into the room. "Tell me then, have you ever been in a relationship that you wanted to get out of?"

I thought about how long I stayed with Jerry, long after the spark was gone. He wasn't a terrible person, he just wasn't my kind of person. At some point, we were just not meant to be together. But I didn't hate him for it.

"Yes. I did want out, and I got out," I told her. "And my life has never been better."

"Ah, see, I knew you'd understand. Sometimes you have to get out of a relationship and then things get better."

I didn't like where this was headed. My eyes darted around the room. What could I do to get away from Wendy? Crawl up a stack of boxes? There was no real way out, except for the passageway that Wendy was blocking.

"What about you and Saundra?" I asked. "You were friends. Did you want out of that relationship? Was she stealing designs from you?"

"Saundra? My friend? Ha! Such a pretentious name, *Saundra*, don't you think? She'll always be Sandy to me—and she was more a business partner than a friend. It had been that way for years. Commerce, plain and simple."

I decided to keep her talking. She'd blocked me into the long narrow room, and she knew it.

"You were both successful. Certainly there couldn't have been any jealousy between you."

"Oh, Jax, you're right, no jealously. But greed, there was plenty of that. And creativity? There wasn't much of that—at least for Sandy. I had plenty of creativity for the both of us."

I kept quiet, trying to figure out what my options were, hoping to keep her talking.

"Did you ever sell something and then wish you hadn't? Did you try to get that something back and have someone stand in your way?"

"I've tried to live without regrets, but it's hard," I said. "What about you?"

"The only regret I have is that I showed you this bracelet. You saw the scratch on my wrist from your damn cat," she said quietly. "You know I was in your room. And you know what? That's fine. When I saw you in the lobby talking with that security guard the night after Saundra died, I knew you were poking around trying to figure out what happened to her. I admit I was trying to scare you, calling you on the phone and telling you to stop it. And destroying your room? That was me just trying to scare you enough so you'd go home and stop trying to figure out who had killed my dear, dear friend," Wendy said with a twist of sarcasm in her voice.

"You know, speaking of friends, I think Tessa's looking for me," I said, hoping that Wendy would let me go if she knew that Tessa would be barging in searching for me at any moment. No such luck.

"I'm going to tell you something I probably shouldn't tell you. But I want someone to know. Someone to understand what it's been like for me all these years."

"Look, Wendy, you don't have to tell me anything. Let's just say goodbye and call it a day. I'm tired, aren't you?" I said, hoping I could derail whatever confession I was about to hear from her. I would much rather that she confess to someone official than to me. Especially since I was feeling vulnerable, trapped in this small room with someone who clearly had murderous intentions.

"Oh Jax, it's okay. I'm going to tell you, and then, like with my dear friend Sandy, I'm going to zap the life right out of you. It worked so well on her, don't you think?"

I knew this for certain: Wendy was riding the crazy train.

"Where do people's creative ideas come from, Jax?"

I stood still, saying nothing.

"Jax, when I ask you a question, you need to answer it." Wendy grabbed a cable from the floor and flung it at me.

I dodged the cable. "From their imagination?" I said.

"Sorry, Jax, that is incorrect. That's a good answer, but not accurate. In Sandy's case, do you want to know where she got her creative ideas? Do you?" Wendy asked, lurching forward. "She got her ideas from *me*."

Wendy pulled on a fist-sized cable hanging from the ceiling. "Oh, what a shame, this one isn't powered up. It's got no juice, no energy. Kind of like my dear friend Sandy. Even before she died, she was dead creatively. Sad but true." Wendy dropped the cable, and we watched it swing back and forth, like a noose on the gallows.

"You don't have to tell me any of this." I didn't want to hear anything more. She was going to confess and then she was going to kill me. That's what crazy killers do to the person they confess to—and I really, really didn't want to be that person.

"Let's try another one now, shall we?" Wendy unclipped the thick black cable from a power box, like the kind I'd had in my booth. "Oh dear, another dead one. It's hard to find a live wire around here," she said, laughing at her cleverness.

"You see, at first it seemed like a terrific idea," Wendy continued, inching toward me. "Sandy paid me for my brilliant designs. I had so many ideas, and she had dried up creatively years ago. She was willing to keep buying my ideas, and I just kept thinking up new things. When I asked you where creative ideas come from, there were a couple of correct answers. One answer: You buy them from a friend. Another answer: You steal them, which is what it seems dear old Sandy did to Minnie, stole a design from that poor young woman.

"I'd been trying to break out of my deal with Sandy for years. I wanted all my designs back. Designs that she'd made her living with, that she'd made thousands of dollars on. I sold her all my best ideas, and what did that leave me? Polka dots. Stupid, boring, crappy polka dots."

"You could have just made your own designs and not worried about whether Saundra made them or not," I said. "You didn't have to just make dots."

"Oh, and have my work be called derivative—copying the work of the great Saundra Jameson? I don't think so. No, no. That simply wasn't possible," said Wendy, moving toward a large metal electrical cabinet with its door ajar, a padlock hanging open on the outside.

"Wendy, seriously, I don't want to hear this. Let's just get out of here, and we'll see if we can clear this up," I said, stepping as far back from her as possible.

"Oh, now, this looks like a live one," Wendy said, reaching inside the cabinet.

Steadying herself, she gripped the cabinet frame and yanked on a well-worn plug. An arc of electricity burst from the panel, lighting up the room with a pulsing release of energy. Like lightning, the flash hit Wendy hard, slamming into her and pushing her backward into a stack of boxes. Screaming, Wendy crumpled to the floor. The room crashed into darkness. I climbed past Wendy and her scooter, staying low to avoid the smoke that was filling the room.

I stumbled through the dark ballroom and found Ryan in the lobby.

"Wendy was electrocuted!" I grabbed Ryan's hand and pulled him into the darkness. He flicked on his flashlight as we ran past the empty tables. We rounded the corner into the utility room. Wendy was lying face-up on the floor, her eyes half-closed, a smoking power cord next to her. The acrid smell of melted wire and burnt skin hung in the air.

I looked closely at Wendy. She was still breathing, but barely.

"Wendy confessed to killing Saundra and tried to kill me, too."

"I'll call for medical help," Ryan said, kneeling next to Wendy.

Leaving Ryan with Wendy, I sprinted through the darkness and into the bright lobby. I found Tiffany in the conference room she'd been using for her chats.

"Detective, we have solved the murder of Saundra Jameson," I said, out of breath.

Tiffany's perfect eyebrows arched in surprise. "I already have the culprits in custody," she said, looking disdainfully at me. "Better luck next time."

"Detective? I think you should go check the utility room," I said. "You'll find the real killer in there."

Tiffany headed into the darkened ballroom.

FORTY-ONE

RYAN AND I WATCHED as a gurney holding Wendy Wilson was pushed through the hotel's back doors by a crew of emergency technicians, followed closely behind by Detective Tiffany Houston.

"I think Detective Houston can handle things from here. Now, Ms. O, may I escort you to your room?" Ryan asked as he wrapped his arm around me.

"My room? Does that mean I can stay another night?"

"Yes, it does," Ryan said as we got into the elevator and pressed the button for the penthouse suite. The doors slid shut, and Ryan reached up and put his hand over the camera so the guards watching the elevator's video stream wouldn't be able to see us. He kissed me, the longest, best kiss I'd ever had.

"That's strange," Ryan said, removing his hand from the camera. "The trapdoor up here by the camera is open. Someone working on the elevator must have forgotten to close it. No wonder it's been so cold in here." He reached up and pulled the small door shut.

Mystery solved. No ghosts here at The Red Rose Hotel.

"But one thing is mysterious. Why does it smell like women's perfume in here?" Ryan asked.

"It's a long story. I'll tell you all about it sometime."

"Would you like to come in?" I asked when we arrived at my room. "Gumdrop went home with Val, and Tessa went with them."

"That means you're alone?" Ryan asked. "Because I have been assigned to keep a close eye on you. A really close eye."

"Do you want to see how close you can get?" I asked.

"Oh, yes, I do," Ryan said as he closed the door behind us. "First we've got to make sure your suite is secure. Let's check the bedroom."

The radio on Ryan's belt crackled to life. "Ryan? It's Marie. We've got a situation down here in reception."

Ryan pressed the button on his radio and responded. "Marie, I'm off duty now."

"No one else is answering. We've got a man, he looks like he's got a gun—"

"Jax, I'm sorry, I've got to go," Ryan said, and not waiting for me to respond, he dashed out the door.

"Goodbye," I said with a sigh as I closed the door behind him. It was going to be a lonely evening. I dug through the mini-bar and found a tiny bottle of champagne and a precious box of Godiva chocolates, then headed toward the bathroom to draw a bubble bath. I was finally going to get my Double Bubbles.

FORTY-TWO

RYAN FOUND ME the next morning while I was putting the last of my show supplies into the trunk of The Ladybug.

"Jax! Great news!"

"I get to spend another night?"

"No, sorry, but I hope you weren't too lonesome last night without me."

"I survived." On champagne and chocolate. "What about the gunman?"

"It was a false alarm. The guy had an umbrella," Ryan said with an exasperated sigh.

"Of course it was. We are in Portland, after all."

"I did some checking into Carl Shulman's background, and he used to work on the security staff at the University of Oregon campus. Detective Houston checked her database, and it looks like Carl may be the guard who turned Miles over to the police when he hit that cop in the face with his protest sign. We're looking at whether Miles was trying to settle that score."

"Ryan?"

"The coroner is looking at a ukulele case as the murder weapon. Can you believe—?"

"Ryan? Can we talk about something else? I'm kind of all murdered-out," I said.

"Of course, sorry," Ryan said. "I just got carried away."

"Will you come up and visit? Seattle's only a few hours away," I said.

"I applied for a position in the Seattle Police Department a few months ago. All I need to do is pass my final exams, and hopefully I'll get hired. With luck, I'll be moving closer to you," Ryan said. "They asked me last week for my references, which means I'm on the short list of candidates. Can I give them your name?"

"Sure, I'm happy to help," I said, wondering if he'd actually move to Seattle some day. It seemed like a long shot.

Ryan pulled me up close and kissed me. "I'll see you again," he said. He let go of me gently, looking at me intensely with those deep, mocha eyes. My whole body felt warm and flushed. I put the top down on The Ladybug so I could cool down, but I didn't think it would help much.

• • •

When I got home, Tessa's car was parked out front. I drove around back and let myself in through the studio. "Tessa? Tessa? Are you here?" I called as I dropped my suitcase at the backdoor.

Gumdrop cruised down the hall toward me.

"Gummie! Are you feeling better after your trip?" I picked up my cat and placed him on the kitchen counter. I pulled a bowl out of one of my cabinets. What was this? New cabinet knobs! My entire kitchen had them, and better still, they were the color of Ryan's eyes. Who had installed these? I was pretty sure I knew who the culprit was: Val.

Gumdrop paced impatiently back and forth across the counter, waiting for his treat, completely unimpressed by my new cabinet hardware. I opened the freezer, flicked a catnip ice cube into the bowl, and placed it on the floor. Gumdrop launched himself off the counter and attacked the catnip cube.

I headed out my front door, then turned and knocked on Val's door. There was a booming bark from the other side of it.

"Val, open up. It's Jax."

"What's the secret password?"

"We don't have one." At least I knew what the password was this time.

"I'm sorry, that is incorrect. I changed my password," Val said through the door. "I heard that it's a good security measure to change your password now and then."

"Open the door right now!"

"Oh, good, you know the new password."

Val opened the door, and Stanley nearly bowled me over. "Stanley, back off," I said, but it was too late. My shoes were already covered in slobber.

"Tessa, I thought I saw your car out front. What are you doing here?"

"Returning Stanley."

"Did you see my present?" Val asked.

"So it was you! Thank you so much. Those knobs are perfect. Where did you get them?"

"At the Saturday Market. I bought them the same day I bought the Cosmos bead, and we were so distracted by the bead, I never got a chance to give you the knobs."

I flopped down on Val's bright pink sofa, resting my head on one of the zebra pillows.

"You're never going to guess what happened after you left," I said.

"Oh, did you and Ryan get a chance for a little horizontal hokey-pokey?" Val asked.

I ignored the question.

"I almost died—nearly got electrocuted. And I found out who Saundra's murderer was."

"We already know who the murderer was, it was Minnie," Tessa said.

"But it's not Minnie. It's Wendy."

"No way! I can't believe it," Tessa said. "And what about Miles?"

"Yeah, but did you get a little nookie?" Val asked.

"I'm not saying."

"Aha! That means yes."

"No, it means I'm not going to talk about it."

"Let me Vulcan Mind Meld you. Please. I can find out without you saying a word."

"No way, Val."

FORTY-THREE

A FEW DAYS LATER, I had a visitor at my front door.

"Detective Grant? What a surprise." I had wondered if the stern detective might stop by again. After our last phone conversation, it sounded like he might. I wasn't sure I wanted to see him, now that I had Ryan in my life. Ryan wasn't exactly in my life, but he had potential, especially if he moved to Seattle.

"Come in," I said. I'd never seen Zachary Grant looking so casual. He looked like a different guy in khakis and a navy polo shirt. And while he looked a little stiff around the edges, he had a sexiness about him I'd never quite seen before.

"Nice to see you again, Jax," Zachary said.

I was glad the house wasn't too much of a train wreck. The dishes had been done, and I'd recently de-furred the sofa and rugs.

"Have a seat here at the kitchen table." I was nervous to have him in my house. Detective Grant had always snarled at me when he could have smiled, and it was only recently that he had shown any signs of warmth. "Thanks for getting rid of the scary guy who was lurking around on our front porch."

"No problem. One of our officers had a talk with him. Turns out he had a couple of priors, so you won't be seeing him again for a while."

"I'll let Val know that she doesn't need to worry about him."

"I suppose you're wondering what I'm doing here," the detective said, taking off his dark-framed glasses and setting them on the table. He went from Clark Kent to Superman by simply removing his glasses.

"Yes, I am. Is this business? Personal?"

"A mixture. Your name popped up in the most unusual way. I was reading some applications for new recruits to the police force…"

I knew where this was headed.

"Did you come across an applicant named Ryan Shaw, by any chance?" I asked.

"As a matter of fact, I did. He lists you as a personal and professional reference."

"I can vouch for him. Very professional. He helped solve a murder at a hotel in Portland."

"And personal?"

"He's a nice guy, an upstanding citizen."

"Just how personal are you talking about?"

"Detective Grant, that's none of your busi—"

"Zachary."

"What exactly are you asking? Does the nature of my relationship with Ryan Shaw have any bearing on his application to the Seattle Police Department?"

"That depends."

"Depends on what?"

"On whether you'd be willing to go out with me if Ryan moved to Seattle."

"Are you asking me out?" Oh dear, life was getting complicated.

"Yes, I suppose I am," said Zachary.

"And Ryan?"

"No, I don't want to go out with him," Zachary said, cracking a smile. "I think he'll be moving up here if he accepts his job offer. And you, do you accept my offer?"

"Yes, I suppose I do."

ACKNOWLEDGMENTS

An enormous thank you to all the amazing early readers of this book. Their help and support have been phenomenal. I'm hoping they'll stick with me for the next book! Thanks to Jim Herrick of Motion Laboratories for sharing his knowledge with me about electrical power distribution systems. A special thank you goes out to Marilyn Peters and JeriLyn Alderman, who together made a real Cosmos bracelet that exists in more than just my imagination.

I'm grateful to Jeff, Kiera, Mom, and all the rest of my loving family and friends, who have supported and encouraged me through this and many of my other crazy creative endeavors. Love you guys.

ABOUT THE AUTHOR

Janice Peacock decided to write her first mystery novel after working in a glass studio full of colorful artists who didn't always get along. They reminded her of the quirky and often humorous characters in the murder mystery books she loves to read. Inspired by that experience, she combined her two passions and wrote *High Strung*, the first book in the Glass Bead Mystery Series featuring glass beadmaker Jax O'Connell. Janice has continued the series with *A Bead in the Hand*, and *Be Still My Beading Heart, A Glass Bead Mini-Mystery*.

When Janice isn't writing about glass artists-turned-amateur-detectives, she creates glass beads using a torch, designs one-of-a-kind jewelry, and makes sculptures using hot glass. Her work has been exhibited internationally and is in the permanent collections of the Corning Museum of Glass, the Glass Museum of Tacoma, WA, and in private collections worldwide.

Janice lives in the San Francisco Bay Area with her husband, two cats, and an undisclosed number chickens. She has a studio full of beads...lots and lots of beads.

CONNECT WITH JANICE PEACOCK

www.JanicePeacock.com
jp@janicepeacock.com
www.blog.janicepeacock.com

Sign up for Janice's newsletter:
www.tinyurl.com/janpeacnewsletter

www.facebook.com/janpeac
Twitter, Instagram: @JanPeac
www.pinterest.com/janpeac
www.JanicePeacockGlass.com
www.etsy.com/shop/janicepeacock

Did you enjoy this book?
Please write a review on the website where you purchased it.

MORE BOOKS IN THE GLASS BEAD MYSTERY SERIES

HIGH STRUNG
Glass Bead Mystery Series
Book 1

After inheriting a house in Seattle, Jax O'Connell is living the life of her dreams as a glass beadmaker and jewelry designer. When she gets an offer to display her work during a bead shop's opening festivities, it's an opportunity Jax can't resist—even though the store's owner is the surliest person Jax has ever met.

The weekend's events become a tangled mess when a young beadmaker is found dead nearby and several oddball bead enthusiasts are suspects. Jax must string together the clues to clear her friend Tessa's name—and do it before the killer strikes again.

BE STILL MY BEADING HEART
A Glass Bead Mini-Mystery

It's Valentine's Day and Jax O'Connell's red VW bug is missing. Did she forget where she parked The Ladybug as she rushed to deliver her handmade glass beads, or has the beloved car been stolen? Searching the streets of Seattle, Jax and her best friend, Tessa, face some unsavory characters. Jax regrets not having a date on the most romantic day of the year after spotting Ryan, Seattle's newest—and hottest—cop and running into Zachary, the stern yet sexy detective. She must take matters into her own hands to find The Ladybug and salvage her love life, and do it before the day is over. This stand-alone short story features the quirky characters of the Glass Bead Mystery Series and is available as an ebook.

OFF THE BEADIN' PATH
Glass Bead Mystery Series
Book Three

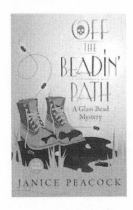

Glass beadmaker Jax O'Connell and her friend Tessa have no idea what challenges await them when they take a glassblowing class with Marco De Luca, a famous Italian glass artist—and infamous lothario.

After the first night of class, Tessa sees a body through the rain-streaked window of the studio. The next morning there's no sign of Marco, and one of the studio owners is also missing. The local sheriff isn't taking the disappearances seriously, but Tessa knows what she saw. To complicate matters, Officer Shaw and Detective Grant are both vying for Jax's attention as she tracks down clues in a small town that's been keeping more than one secret.

Jax and Tessa must face their fears to find the body and uncover the killer before another life is shattered.